INDIGO HAZE 2

Thug Love is the Best Love

AUBREÉ PYNN

B. Love Publications

INTRODUCTION

To the reader:

Before you even get started, there's a few things I need to tell you about. This is a ride. A ride that might make you cry. A ride that might make you smile and be hopeful. I ask that you do a few things for me and for yourself before you dive into Indigo Haze. This is the second installment of this series. I highly suggest you read part one before cracking this open.

Please leave a review, I need to hear how you felt, please don't leave any spoilers in your review, and last but not least by a long shot, if you have lost any loved ones due to gun violence please proceed with caution. This body of work may trigger you.

Remember, my inbox is open for you to vent!
Until the end, much love,

- A.P.

PREFACE

Grief is the final act of love...

UNTITLED

I live for your love
I'll never get enough
Until heaven comes to take me up
You'll be all I'm living for
You own my heart
It only beats for you
And when you're gone it'll stop

- Candice Glover: Die Without You

PROLOGUE

T aj Ali Sims

Four Years Later

"Baby, what do you want to do with your life?" Bubba's voice was even and calm. Even after the two of them had argued most of the way to get burgers and shakes for dinner since Senior was working a double.

Taj's brows pushed together at Bubba's sudden change of tone. She was still furious with him but that wasn't going to stop her from responding to him.

"Not be a nurse or anything else Senior wants me to do. I want to own a coding company full of beautiful, bold, brilliant, black women. There are not enough of us involved in STEM programs. I want to change the way the tech industry looks and the way young girls see it."

There was nothing more Bubba enjoyed than watching how her face lit up when she talked about her future and her dreams. One thing he knew about Taj, outside of her being stubborn as a mule, was that she was smart as hell. Whatever she put her mind to, she could do and would do. And if anyone said otherwise, she made it her mission to prove them wrong. She was determined like that. Determined to make anything and everything work in her favor. That was why he fought so hard for her. She was too smart to be getting caught up with some lame ass niggas from around the way. Niggas felt like they could try Taj because she was beautiful and Bubba was her brother. They got off from the thrill and not because they wanted to really know who she was. After her last incident with a lame, he wasn't having any more of that shit. He didn't care if the nigga had true feelings for her or not. No one was going to be in her presence, looking for an easy pass or clout.

"Baby, you're smart as fuck. You're pretty as fuck. Niggas will try to ruin that shit for you. They're going to be stuck here all of their lives and you're not. They hate that shit. They're going to look for a reason to test you. Keep minding your business."

Taj huffed. Although she knew that Bubba was one hundred percent right, it didn't take away from the fact that eventually, she would want someone who wasn't her brother or her father to love and protect her.

"So, I'm supposed to be an old biddy forever."

"Nah, not forever. There's some nigga out there who is going to love you and protect you and all that other shit. But it ain't right now, though. You're graduating as Valedictorian in a month. Fuck these niggas, Baby. You got a whole lot of shit to do and adding a nigga in that mix is going to distract you."

"All right," she said, looking out the window of his Honda Civic. "Just when it happens, don't beat him up, please."

"Baby, you crazy as hell thinking I'm not gonna touch him. I gotta see if that nigga got heart or not. Ain't no niggas going to be around you with no heart, no backbone, no code. That's dead." Bubba snickered and peeped over to Taj, who had her brows pushed closer together. *"Baby, you got something in you worth protecting. That shit is special. Shit is going to happen to you. Shit is going to test you. It's not on you, it's in you. Keep your feet planted and you'll get through anything. Remember to always dream as big as you want. You can go places and do things and touch people. You got the torch, so run with that shit."*

It was heavy. Her heart, her spirit, the space surrounding her and the space she tried to settle in but couldn't find home in it. Her face should have worn a smile, but it didn't budge. It couldn't. The muscles in her face simply refused to show anything but angst. For the last four years, Taj rarely felt moments of joy, and when she did, she immediately felt guilty for feeling. How dare she feel when Bubba couldn't and neither could Indie?

Bubba and Indie.

The mere thought of them caused her heart to sink and a sharp pain to course from her heart to her gut, again. It was one thing to miss Bubba the way she did. She had to miss him. Bubba was the flesh of her flesh and blood of her blood. It was only right that she did. But Indie was different. The pain of losing him hit her differently. The closure surrounding that loss was different. She loved him outside of the surface. Everything he was and had the potential to be was what wrecked her. Their souls connected with one another and didn't give so much as a warning that it was happening. It just did. As soon as it happened, she lost it.

Although their time together was short, it was everything she needed and everything she never knew she needed. Unbeknownst to Indie, he saved her life, not just physically, but the love and the affection he offered renewed her spirit. And because of that, she would have to carry that forever. She lived every day knowing that he loved her, too. The simple act of shielding her made Indie's place in her heart a permanent fixture. She'd held on to the memory of him tightly, and letting him go would mean that he was gone for good. She couldn't come to terms with that. Since losing him, she had to tell herself that Indie wasn't here, but he was here. She cradled him within the depths of her spirit and tattooed his name in ink next to the blue anchor on her wrist. Everyone would know that Indigo Sims was a part of who she was then and the reason behind who she was now.

Feeling Ricky's hands grip her shoulders and massage them roughly, she pulled herself out her thoughts with reluctance. When she was consumed with thoughts of him, she didn't want to let them go.

"What are you doing sitting over here by yourself? This is your graduation party. Put a smile on your face, cuz. Look around, even Senior is smiling."

A faint smile crossed her lips but that was it. She couldn't force herself to give any more than that. Ricky's eyes grew sad for her while he examined his Baby's face. He wanted to tell her the truth so bad, but he couldn't bring himself to upset her on her day or betray Indie's trust. He almost wanted to force Indie out of hiding so her disposition could change. Instead of spilling the tea all over the table, he looked around her tiny apartment and let a sigh escape his lips.

Taj licked her dry lips and spoke. "Ricky."

Turning his head back to face her, he replied. "What's up?"

"How do you ...you know... handle this loss? He was your best friend and you seem fine. Maybe it's me, I know it's been four years and I should get over it, but how?" She looked up at Ricky with her big eyes filled with sorrow. Ricky hummed and took a seat by her. "I feel guilty as hell for being happy...like how dare I be happy when —"

"Baby, you know that man loved you, right?" Ricky questioned and watched as Taj nodded her head. "He would want you to be happy. Everything you got right now, is everything he wanted for you and more. There's no guilt in that. Even Bubba would want you to be happy. I know if they were here, they would be so proud of everything you've done and everything you're going to do."

Taj let out a heavy sigh and blinked a few tears away from her eyes.

"I miss them, but today, I miss them more. I keep telling myself not to look up in the crowd tomorrow because they won't be there."

Ricky rubbed his hands across his jeans and sucked in a deep breath. Watching Taj go through this was hard for him. It took so much for him to stand by and watch as she bounced back and forth with her emotions for years. Even after rounds of therapy, she still wasn't completely okay with everything. But who would be? She watched the tragic end of people she loved. The hardest thing for Ricky to do was watch her process and know that if Indie came back home, all of this emotion would go away. Her infectious smile might return, her process would strengthen and her love would no longer be caged inside of a corridor of her lonely heart.

"Indie never left you. Bubba never left you. That love they had for you was real. So real that it lives on even after they're gone. If you think that they're not watching over you, you're crazy. Remember...it's in you..."

"Not on you. Thank you, Ricky," Taj hummed, turning her body to wrap her arms around his midsection.

"Baby, I got you. I always will. Don't forget that shit," Ricky grunted and kissed the top of her head through her hair. "Now, wipe your face, stop that pouting girl and let's take a shot or two."

Indigo "Indie" Sims

Pauley's Pavilion was packed with smiling faces and joy bounced from wall to wall. The sea of people flowing into their seats were happily waiting to cheer for their loved ones and express how happy they were for them. The graduating class was due to march in soon, making the anxiety rise in Indie's chest as he traveled to the top of the arena to find a seat in the corner by himself. The view wasn't the best but it would keep him out of sight from any potential danger that could be lingering around. By now, everyone probably settled down, but he could never be caught slipping again. Being here, in LA, was already a risk.

Since he recovered from his near-death experience, he'd been laying low as possible. Anything he did in Oakland always went through three people before it got back to him. It made his hustle complicated since he didn't have his ears to the ground like he was used to, but it worked for him and it kept him safe. He'd only been back to Los Angeles to lay his eyes on her every so often and leave. Ricky and his mother kept him up to date on everything. But seeing Taj graduate from college with honors was worth every single risk. Her dreams were worth his life.

He was so proud of her; words couldn't describe how much his heart burst with happiness. Her tenacity, her resilience, and her ability to overcome the most traumatic experiences of her life made his soul smile. Indie didn't expect anything less from her. She was born to shine and prevail through anything. It was embedded in her DNA. Whether she knew it or not, he did.

Sitting in his seat, he looked down and around to see if he could spot Senior. He couldn't. He knew how much Taj meant to him, especially now that she was his only living child. Senior would do whatever he had to do to make sure he protected that. Indie understood that, which was why he'd kept his distance from her. Sometimes he wished he never interrupted her light with his, but her light, love, and stillness was something that he needed.

The band started to play the music to march the graduating class in and he pulled himself out of his thoughts and peered down at the graduates intently. It wasn't hard to find Taj. Her curls made it almost impossible for her cap to fit over them. But in true Taj fashion, she always made it work.

He watched as she took her seat and looked as she scanned over the sea of people to find Senior and Ms. Mary. Once she spotted them, her somber expression faded into a soft smile. Indie spotted Senior and Mary side by side and smirked happily. Taj turned her head back to the front, facing the stage. Her cap was decorated with two blue hearts and cursive words between them that read *Indigo Dreamin'*.

His heart sank, his eyes fluttered and his breathing grew shallow. All he wanted was to run down the stands and tell her she didn't have to be sad anymore. She didn't have to cry or wonder about the what if's anymore. He was here and he was ready to love her the way she deserved to be loved. Indie imagined himself tilting her chin upward into the light and placing a kiss to her sweet lips. He wanted to take her pain away, to wrap her in his arms and restore her faith in him and in God. But he couldn't, and it killed him.

As the ceremony went on, she got her degree and held it tightly in her hands. Before she walked off the stage, she stopped briefly to look toward the ceiling and blew two kisses upward toward the sky. One for him and the other for her brother. As she stepped off the stage, her head dropped and she wiped a few tears from her face. Indie's eyes swelled up and his lip trembled. He was never one to wipe them, so he let one fall.

Once the ceremony was over, families had gathered in various places to hug their graduates and take pictures. Indie stood off and watched Taj hug Ms. Mary and her father. Her hug around Senior's neck was tight. He rubbed her back and whispered how proud of her he was for sticking to what she set out to do. Once she pulled away, she wiped her face, chuckled and exhaled.

The need to hug her tenderly was increasing along with his heart rate. The need to bury his face in her hair and inhale her scent was making his hands shake. He needed to feel her skin on his skin and her breath against his lips. There was nothing else like it. There was no one else for him but Taj. In the four years they spent apart, he looked for her in women who could never measure up. Everyone was a knockoff, counterfeit love compared to what he found in her. No one had that light. Although he could look at her and see that her light was dim, it was still there. It was still flickering and it was waiting on his touch to come back and cultivate it.

That was all he needed to see. He was supposed to drive back to Oakland tonight but decided to get a room instead. He was going to step out of the boundaries he created and visit her in a couple of days. He couldn't stomach that look on her face any longer. It was time to come out of hiding. He missed her and he knew that she missed him with every fiber of her being. He could feel it coursing through his being. Her energy was heavy and no matter how hard she fought for it to return to what it once was, it wouldn't. It could never until he turned that flicker into a fire that burned and spread at a dangerous speed.

Her heart was shattered into pieces and he knew that the

only person who could put it back together was him. He was going to do it, but at what cost? Could he love her correctly and still live under the radar? Only time would tell, but right now he needed to be in her space and put his hands on her, even if it were for a moment. He needed to feel her light, be around it and in it.

A couple of days passed by and he finally stopped going back and forth with himself about seeing her. There was no time like the present, and he needed to end this separation now. He sat outside of the apartment a few times before, but today was going to be different. Parking his car on the far end of the parking lot, Indie used the back entrance of the apartment to climb up the stairs to her floor.

He held a bouquet of blue hydrangeas and white tulips in one hand and the other knocked on the door. While he waited patiently, Indie recited his lines over and over and then kissed his teeth. "Nigga, you trippin'. Playas don't sweat shit like this. But playa's ain't never did shit like this, either."

His emotions were high and he needed to settle them before he laid his eyes on her. Before he had to explain why the hell he let her suffer for so long. He knocked again and nothing. Hearing someone climbing up the stairs slowly, he glanced over his shoulder to see an older man with a huge ring of keys in his hand. He must've been the landlord. "You lost, young man?"

Indie shook his head. "Nah, I was just hoping to surprise an old friend."

"Who Taj? She moved out a few days ago."

"Shit," he grumbled to himself, feeling defeated. He hadn't lost track of her in four years and now he had no idea where she was or where she was going. "Do you know where she went?"

"No, she didn't say." The landlord stopped to study him. Indigo turned around to fully face him and scowled a bit. "Who did you say you were?"

"I didn't." Indie's shoulders slumped slightly, catching himself. He stood up straight like everything was cool. Inside of him was anything but. "Thanks. Ay, you got a wife?"

The landlord nodded. Indie handed over the bouquet of flowers he was holding with regret. "Give these to her. I have no need for them. Have a good day."

"You, too. You seem nice. I hope you get in contact with her."

Indie returned to his car to see Ricky leaning on the hood. His brisk walk slowed down to almost an instant halt. Scratching the back of his neck, he groaned to himself and checked their surroundings before proceeding to walk over to Ricky.

Once he reached his car, he leaned on the other side, keeping his eyes on the apartment building while Ricky kept his eyes on the entrance of the apartment complex.

"You're out in the daylight. What's that about, nigga?"

Indie scoffed softly and scratched his unshaven face. "You following me now?"

"I wasn't until I spotted you moving through the crowd at graduation. You're getting sloppy with this shit now," Ricky shared. His tone was more concerned than annoyed. Ricky and Senior were the only ones close enough to Taj to hold on to this secret. Senior did it effortlessly because he didn't want Taj with him anyway, but Ricky knew, and because he knew, it was difficult keeping this information locked away. "What would have happened if she saw you?"

"I could come out of fucking hidin' and tell her I fucked up. I'm getting tired of this shit."

"This is the shit you asked for, nigga. We doing this shit because of you." Ricky kissed his teeth and dropped his head for a second.

Indie groaned and palmed his face. "What you doin' here, Ricky?"

"You need to tie up any loose ends you have in Oakland and come home."

Indie turned to look at Ricky over his shoulder. "For what?"

"The hood ain't the same without you, nigga. We need you. Niggas dying over bullshit," Ricky explained followed by a heavy sigh. "You made niggas want to change and now that you're gone, they back into their old ways."

Indie scoffed and rubbed his hand over the back of his neck. "Look, why the fuck should I care about them niggas after they tried to kill me?"

"Because that's who you are. You're Indigo. You don't have that name just because it's pretty. You got that name because you stand for something. Niggas need you. Joey needs you."

Hearing Joey's name made Indie stand to his feet and turn to face Ricky fully. Ricky stood up and headed toward his car. "Tie up your shit. You got a month to bring your ass home. You don't want me to come and get you."

Indie let out a huff of frustation and opened the door to his car. A month was all he needed to sell the rest of the product he had in Oakland. He was going to throw his cousin a stack for letting him lay low there and when the city slept, he'd pull back in.

The time had come. It was time to come back home and face the music and clean up the mess he made.

UNTITLED

No such thing as a life that's better than yours
Heart beatin' fast let a nigga know that he alive
Fake niggas, mad snakes
Snakes in the grass let a nigga know that he arrived
Don't be sleepin' on your level
'Cause it's beauty in the struggle

- J.Cole: Love Yourz

❦ I ❧

T aj Ali Adams

Two Months Later

Her spirit wasn't light but it wasn't heavy. It hadn't been light in years, but somehow, she managed to smile and move through life. She was visible enough not to have people question her, but not present. Every relationship she had was only surface. Except with Maria. Maria knew. But outside of that, no one else picked up on it. They just wrote Taj off as being closed off. No one understood that her light was dim and the only thing that kept her going was the promise she made to Bubba and Indigo. She had to dig deep to find the strength to keep going.

Day's like today made it hard for her to do that. It was Indigo's birthday and she spent each birthday the same way, holding on to memories of that summer that changed her forever. She never loved anyone the way she loved him. No one saw her the way he saw her. That shit molded her. It chipped away at the shell of her heart and made her appreciate the moments she had.

Standing at the edge of the floor and staring out the window, she peered over the sun setting on the San Francisco Bay. Her arms were wrapped around herself as she clenched her eyes shut, shaking the flashbacks of their last moments away. She found it funny that even though he was gone, she still felt him everywhere.

There were moments that passed when she felt like he was close and watching over her. His protection was everywhere, but she couldn't reach out and touch it. She longed to smell his cologne mixed with a fresh smoked blunt in the knit of his shirt. She longed to trace his tattoos with the tips of her fingers and feel his warmth. Since Indie, she'd had a few lovers, but no one compared. No man had been able to penetrate the walls she built around her heart.

Although she loved Indigo with her life, she vowed that she would never take her heart again. She lost is all not once, but twice. Taj knew that a third time was bound to kill her. She was tired of loving only to lose it. So love wasn't on her criteria list for a partner. She didn't need anyone to love her. She had that part covered on her own. She just needed someone there.

Since her Sophomore year in college, she'd been hustling and saving every penny to pour back into her business. She used the money that Bubba and Indigo left her to secure her business license, trademark, and few computers to start with. Now that she fully made the move to San Francisco, her workspace was secured and she had three employees working full time for her. A website designer, an IT specialist, and Maria. Maria was determined to stay by her side regardless of what state she was in. Because Taj would never ask, but Maria knew she needed her to stay sane.

Taj decided to name her business BOLDnBLUE. It was a very public tribute to her passion, her love for her brother and her love for Indigo and all that they were. Everything she did for the last four years was an outward expression of her love for them.

Every room of her home was painted indigo with white trim. The furniture throughout the house was gray with silver accents and paintings that reflected the world she lived in. Los Angeles skylines, sunsets, and the haze over the city. Taj would always love Los Angeles because Los Angeles gave her Indigo. But she was happy to leave. She needed a break from being reminded of him everywhere she looked. Hopefully, this way she could focus on her building her new life while holding on to his memory.

Her eyes began to flutter while she was flooded with the urge to feel him wrap his arms around her. Just as the tears were getting ready to drop from her eyes, she felt a set of strong arms wrap around her and a gentle kiss was placed to her cheek. It brought her out of her moment. Opening her eyes, she exhaled and forced a smile on her face.

Malcolm Stewart.

A man that she took a liking to enough to distract her from wanting Indigo every moment of the day. He looked nothing like him, smelled nothing like him, but he reminded her of Bubba. Malcolm was medium built with mocha hued skin. He lacked the street knowledge that both Bubba and Indie had, but she didn't think about that much. It was probably a good thing. She couldn't lose him to the streets because he knew nothing about them. Malcolm didn't make her core tighten or make her lose her breath, but he was safe and square. She attempted to fit into those four walls to the best of her ability.

Malcolm was bright and a borderline genius when it came down to technology. He held the same passion for computer science that she did, which made it a lot easier for her to be comfortable with him. Since being paired together in a project their sophomore year, she acknowledged that she was comfortable in his presence. Malcolm had confessed his love for her after meeting Senior at an award ceremony. Of course, wanting her to shed her layer of pain away and move on, Senior pushed her into spending more time with him.

Unfortunately, the woman Malcolm thought he had, wasn't the woman Taj was. The woman he had was emotionally unavailable and used sex every now and then to feel something and release her frustrations. But Malcolm didn't know he could never have the innermost parts of her heart. He thought she was reserved naturally, only opening up when she wanted to or when liquor was involved. Fortunately for her, Malcolm didn't require much effort to stay around. Although she hoped that he would find a reason to leave, he didn't, and she found herself in a relationship with him for the last two years. Not for love, but for the convenience of having someone around her.

"What are you over here thinking about?" His voice irritated her because it ruined her moment. She didn't want to be touched unless it was from Indie. She wanted to stand here and consume her thoughts with memories of the past. If she got lost in her thoughts, she could feel his light. Its warmth and its radiating love she could feel in the moment had Malcolm just let her stay there.

Shrugging herself out his hold, she stepped away and released a sigh.

"Nothing. Just going over tomorrow in my head."

Malcolm sighed and hummed lowly. He slid his hands inside his pockets and watched her move around the room. He knew that every day this year, she got like this, but she never talked about it with him. Taj just claimed it was a moment and it would pass, but as of lately, her moments had been more and more frequent, along with her distance from him. All he wanted to do was hold her and try to take away whatever it was that was bothering her.

"I wish you would tell me what happens inside when you go silent. Where you go..." Malcolm trailed off and blew his breath. He was a patient man and loved Taj, so he was willing to wait forever. "I picked up dinner from that Thai place we spotted a few days ago."

"Go ahead and eat. I'm going to lie down."

"You sure?"

She nodded. "I'm sure. I'll eat it for lunch or something."

Malcolm studied her a little longer before he took a step back and left the room, leaving her alone. Taj fell into her pillows and pulled the covers over her head. A few tears escaped and she prayed that she could see Indigo in her dreams.

She whispered, "Just one more time..."

UNTITLED

Said he grew up in a house and it was love missing
Said he grew up in the set, he keep his guns with him
Young nigga, young nigga
Young nigga, just a young nigga
And he don't need a reason, he a young nigga
And you don't want your daughter and your sons with him.

-Nipsey Hussle: Young Niggas

≈ 2 ≈

I ndie

HE WAS BACK in South Central and it made his stomach turn.
His mind was racing and his chest was tightening again. Indie
never suffered from anxiety until someone decided to put a
price on his head. While he was away in Oakland, he tried not
to think about all the shit happening here, and for a while, he
could. But now that he was back, that night played over and
over in his mind. His shoulders hiked, his stomach tightened
and his leg bounced nervously.

Creeping to the stop sign, he scanned the area with a curl of
his top lip. The hood was still the hood and niggas were still doing
the same shit. Corners were clustered with dope boys, and each
side of the street was separated by the colors they represented and
the sets they claimed. He grumbled something under his breath
and rubbed his forehead, trying to relax just a bit. Niggas were

still up to the same shit and it didn't surprise him. No one wanted to change, but they would complain when someone got shot and talked about it for a few months. By the time the body was cold or the wounds were healed, they were back on their bullshit.

Indie arrived at his old house and parked the car on the curb. Observing the area, he noticed two cars in the driveway. Assuming that one had to be Ajai's, he killed the engine and pushed himself out of the car. The only thing on his mind was to find out what the hell Joey had been up to and why it was so important that he came back. It had to be serious for Ricky to summon him back to L.A.

Walking up the narrow driveway past Ricky's car, he pulled the hood further over his face. He wasn't ready for anyone to know that he was back. Right now, only Ricky needed to know he was here. Word would spread like wildfire and he wasn't ready to explain anything to anyone. Ricky moved into Indie's old spot with Indie's persistence about it shortly after he made his way to Oakland. Indie knew that without him around to keep Ricky straight that he was going to fall back into the streets again. He wanted him to have some-where to lay his head without the threat of someone coming after him. It eased his nerves a little to know that there was still some respect left for him in the hood because it seemed that the house was the same way he left it.

Stopping at the front door, he pounded his fist on the it and swallowed the lump on his throat. He was home, but every-thing felt so foreign to him. The sound of chains falling off the locks made him take a step back and wait for Ricky to say something.

"Who that?" Ricky called from the other side.

"Nigga...you know who this is," Indie replied, hearing the doorknob turn before Ricky pulled the door open. Reaching out to give Indie a handshake, Ricky pulled him into a hug. "You act like you missed me, nigga. What you been up to?"

"Ain't shit. Happy to have you back, nigga!" Ricky cheered, stepping back so he could fully walk into the house.

The house had a woman's touch, so he knew that Ajai made herself at home, too.

"What's goin' on around here? Where is Ajai?"

"Over at her mommas with your nephew. She'll be back soon. She made some food; you hungry?"

Indie shook his head and pulled his hoodie off. Walking past him with two bottles of water, Ricky handed one to Indie. "So, tell me what you want first, the good news or the bad news?"

Indie pressed his lips together and went to sit down on the couch. Resting his elbows on his knees, he looked at Ricky and anxiously waited to hear what he had to say. Since all of it had to do with Joey, he braced himself. No matter how Ricky flipped it, it would still be bad news.

Indie grunted. "Just tell me what the fuck is going on. What I needed to leave Oakland for?"

"Nigga, don't even start acting like you had a whole life in Oakland." Ricky smacked his lips and dropped into the other chair and ran his hand over his low fade. "Don't tell me you did, either."

"A few bitches and a hustle, but nothing to really talk about."

"How long have I heard that shit?" Ricky chuckled lightly and then sighed. "You didn't leave no kids behind, did you?"

Indie kissed his teeth and waved Ricky off. "I never do. So, cut to it. What the fuck is up?"

"A couple of things have changed since you been out the mix. TK promoted me and Joey is...was running for me, which —"

"Hold up, hold up. Repeat that, nigga." Indie sat up more and stared at Ricky with a furrowed brow. "I didn't hear you correctly."

"Indie, I had my eyes on him." Ricky defended, still looking for the right words to tell Indie about his brother. When it came to his family, there were no right words. Ricky knew whatever reaction Indie would have to the news would be warranted.

"Why you keep talking in past tense, nigga? What the fuck you mean he *was* running for you? Who the fuck is he running for now? Better yet, how long has he been back in this gang shit? And I could have sworn I asked you to keep an eye on him!" Indie fired off. His light brown face was now burning red with frustration and a hint of anger. He was mad enough to blow steam out his nose.

Ricky's body language screamed that he didn't want to tell Indie how everything happened. Joey should have been graduating from high school by now, but instead, he was too deep in some gang shit. Indie's mind started to race, and when it stopped for a moment, landed on his mother. He knew that she was probably going through it. She didn't like that Indie was bangin' when he was, but Joey, she was probably sick over it.

It was one thing for Ricky to submerge himself back into that life, but not Joey. His concern shifted from how Ricky was maintaining to how the hell he could get Joey out, again. Indie couldn't save him. Joey was hellbent about getting back in the gang life when Indie was finally out of sight and out of mind. He wanted to be pissed off with Ricky, but at the end of the day, he knew the blame rested on his shoulders. Although Ricky and Indie were close like brothers, Joey and Indie were blood and Joey was always Indie's responsibility.

"A couple of years. It wasn't a problem until now. I mean, I couldn't keep the little nigga from falling into your shoes, but I could at least keep my eye on him. Joey has been pulling away

from me, though, and doing whatever the fuck he wants to do,"
Ricky muttered, hoping that Indie's cool demeanor would
remain intact, but that was asking a lot of him. "He's off the
fuckin' handle and you need to reign him back in before your
momma loses a son for real."

With a shake of his head and agitated grunt, Indie looked at
Ricky and asked, "Why the fuck would he pull away from you?
Like, what else is there to get into but the same shit you in?"

"I ain't killin' niggas." Ricky spoke up, automatically making
Indie's scowl intensify with annoyance. "I'm just a drug dealer.
That's it. That young nigga wants to run shit like the Wild
Wild West."

"Tell me this." Indie's red face held its color but his tone was
still even and collected. "Why would you even let him get back
into this shit in the first place?"

"Nigga," Ricky scoffed. "You ghosted his ass. Fucka, you
ghosted everyone! Me, your moms, Joey! You were supposed to
make sure he was cool. What that fuck I look like?"

"Like my fucking brother who's supposed to pick up where
I fell short at. What the fuck you mean what the fuck you look
like, nigga? Right now, you lookin' weird as fuck to me. Don't let
that little promotion get back to your head. And how the fuck
you even..."

Ricky groaned and tried to shake Indie's attitude off, but he
couldn't.

"I worked my ass off, nigga! I had to. I never had half the
fucking opportunities you did! You liked to throw those motiva-
tional speeches around about getting the fuck out of here. But
how? I ain't out here building computers and stacking bread."

"Nigga, you full of fucking excuses. You know that," Indie
groaned. "I didn't come back here to argue with you."

The air in the room was tense. Indie fell back in the cushions and looked at the ceiling. He could never be mad at Ricky

for long. Although he was irritated with the situation, it was no one's fault that Joey was deeply involved in the gang life but his. He didn't give anyone much of a choice when he left. And now that he was back, he had to face the music of his actions, and that started with Joey.

"It ain't on you, nigga," Indie finally broke through the tension. "All this shit is on me. I ran away and this is what I got to deal with. Joey bangin', your back against the wall and..."

Indie's thoughts trailed off to Taj. His heart sank and a low rumble escaped his lips. She was the one that got away and the one he needed back. She was the piece to the puzzle that made him complete. Even after four years, he still wanted to be consumed by her. Every woman he found himself entertaining could never measure up to Taj. A long heavy sigh reset his thoughts and he refocused.

"It's on both of us. You left it up to me and I dropped that ball. But it ain't too late to turn this shit around," Ricky spoke up.

Indie nodded and sprung to his feet. "You right. I'll be back."

"You need me to ride?" Ricky asked, standing up. Indie shook his head and opened the front door.

"I got it."

﷼ 3 ﷼

J oseph "Joey" Sims

His mom was working the night shift and that gave him the opportunity to do whatever the hell it was that he wanted to do. The streets were quiet tonight, so there wasn't much to get into but some pussy, and that was what was on the top of his list. Once he was done with that, he would spark up and chill for the rest of the night.

Joseph walked into the house with Sonya, a fine ass girl from around the way that he had his eyes on. She was the typical girl that most of the hood niggas went after, light skin and pretty hair. She was one of the girls everyone swore he would never get. Funny how things had seemed to work out for them. At first, she really didn't want anything to do with him. Joey was just a nerdy kid with a slick mouth and terrible game. But the second word got out that he was affiliated, her interest piqued. When she decided to come around and show her interest, Joey didn't pay her much mind, but it wasn't until a light bulb went off in his head.

She wanted to be down just to say that she was rolling, and Joey wanted some pussy. It was an easy fix for him at least. He had no intention of making her anything more than what she was now, a good time.

Flicking the lights on, he heard a steady rhythmic noise from the back of the house. He glared at Sonya and gritted his teeth. "You trying to set me up or some shit?"

She responded no higher than a whisper. "Why would I want to do that, Joey?"

He cut his eyes at her and pulled his gun from the waist of his pants.

"Stay right there, don't move."

Sonya released a low sigh and sat on the couch. Joey was a good shot so she felt okay with the situation. No one had ever gotten a leg up on him yet and tonight wasn't going to be the night. Plus, there wasn't any niggas dumb enough in the hood to come to where his mother laid her head.

Joey slowly inched down the hall and the noise steadily continued. It was coming from Indie's room. He hadn't been in there since he left. Joey's feelings surrounding the situation was anything but acceptance. He wasn't okay with his brother leaving, and probably would never be. He felt like Indie made the worst move by running away. He should have stayed and gone to war with them niggas. In Joey's eyes, Indie was just as much of a coward as their father. When shit got too hard, he ran. Indie did the same thing.

Stopping at Indie's door, he squinted into the crack of the door to see Indie sitting on the edge of his bed, bouncing his old basketball. Joey's heart dropped into the pit of his stomach. His eyes grew wide and he swallowed the lump in his throat. Even with the anger he had toward him surrounding his abrupt departure, Joey missed his brother and all he ever wanted to do was be like him. Instead of going into the room to embrace his brother, he pushed the door open with his foot and aimed the gun at Indie.

Expecting Indie to be shaken by his action, he was surprised when he said, "If you thinking about shooting me, nigga, make sure you take me out. I don't know if you heard or not, I don't die."

Joey involuntarily let a chuckle escape his lips and dropped the gun to his side.

"Fuck you doing here, nigga? Ain't you supposed to be in Oakland hiding and shit?"

"Fuck you doing with a gun, nigga? Ain't you supposed to be graduating high school and shit?" Indie retorted, looking up at his little brother who wasn't so little anymore.

Joey had facial hair and he was about three feet taller than Indie remembered. It was like Indie was looking into a mirror. He stood to his feet and stepped to his brother. Joey didn't flinch. He held his head high like Indie was a nigga off the street and not his flesh and blood.

Indie trailed his eyes from the top of Joey's head to his feet. Crisp white shirt, blue jeans, a blue flag on his left side and blue chucks.

"So, you really 'bout it, huh, nigga? Fly crippin' and shit?"

Joey scoffed with laughter and scanned his eyes over Indie, who had on the same exact outfit. "Ain't you? Nah, not like you. You ran the fuck away like a bitch."

Indie took a step back and rubbed his forehead. "You everything like me, nigga."

"I ain't nothing like you, nigga. Everything that happens to me, I confront that shit head on. You a weird ass nigga that claims the set and runs when shit gets tough."

"Nigga," Indie scoffed, ready to separate Joey's head from his shoulders. "Who the fuck are you talking to like that?"

"Ain't nobody in here but us, nigga. You a bitch." Joey snarled. Before he could make another comment, Indie had him by his throat and jolted into the wall. Joey grunted. "Get the fuck off of me."

"Nah, I'm a bitch, nigga? That's what we calling it now? If I would have stayed, it would have been a war. Unlike you, I know the value of life and ain't no one I love dying because of me."

"So, you run and have everyone think you're dead? That was smart," Joey grunted sarcastically, pushing Indie off of him. "That shit don't mean shit to me."

"So, I leave and you get down with TK after all that shit I did to get your dumbass out. This ain't the life you supposed to have, nigga! You're wasting your life."

Joey looked at his brother and smirked. "And you did, too. Look at you, nigga. What you got to show for the last four years? Nothing. Someone had to keep food on the table and the bills paid in this bitch, so I stepped up. Say thank you."

"You keep talking like this, your little life is going to get fucked up in the worst way."

"Look around, it's already fucked up, and that's on you."

Indie tried his best not to go off and lunge at Joey again. He shook his head and shoved his hands in his pockets.

"Aight, nigga. So TK was your last result? Fuck you doing with that nigga?"

Joey laughed and said. "I got a piece of pussy waiting on me in the living room. I ain't getting into this shit. You can either stay or leave. But we done with this shit."

"Answer my question," Indie rumbled. "Pussy can wait. We havin' a man to man conversation."

"It's best that you don't know. Get out of here before

someone sees you. I'm not in the mood to explain your reappearance. Neither do I feel like shootin' a nigga tonight. Even if he's my brother."

Indie threw his hands up and gave Joey an amused look.

"I'm not going far. I'll see you later."

Joey watched as Indigo left out the front door and disappeared down the street. Glancing over at Sonya, he closed the door and nodded to his room. Indie ruined his mood. He tried to regain it, but it was all gone. Sonya even noticed that he wasn't present. She smacked her lips and climbed off his lap.

"Nigga, I'm not doing this. When you get your head out of the clouds, call me."

Joey didn't reply. He didn't even budge while she huffed and puffed and stormed out of the house. His brother was home. He was happy he was home, and worried for him at the same time.

"Indie should have stayed where he was," Joey muttered to himself, locking the front door. Joey knew that Indigo's dreams were too big for this place. They wanted to kill that dream, and the best way to do it was to kill him.

Guilt fell on Joey's shoulders replaying everything that just went down with him and Indie. There was a time when he looked up to Indie and wanted to be just like him. But four years without him, he had to learn to look up to himself. He had to figure out how he was going to navigate through all this bullshit by himself. He didn't want Ricky in his business, but although Joey was down with the set, he had other shit to tend to. The reason he was so deep into the life was bigger than him. He loved his brother and his mother, and he hated the look on his mom's face and hated the fact that his brother had to leave the place he called home.

Rolling up a blunt, Joey lit up and smoked the night away. He needed to relax so he could sleep a couple of hours. The weed wasn't doing anything but making his mind race more. Now that Indie was back, the threat of him ruining everything that he worked for while he was away lingered. Giving up his need for sleep, Joey was now fueled with the need to keep his brother off the radar and his plan intact without Indie or Ricky catching on to his true motive.

UNTITLED

You are but a phoenix among feathers
You're broken by the waves among the sea
They'll let you die, they'll let you wash away
But you swim as well as you fly
- SZA: Pretty Little Birds

﷽ 4 ﷽

T aj

Legs tucked under her butt, curls falling freely wherever they wanted to and her favorite drink in her hand, Taj was fully prepared to enjoy her night in with Maria. They had tacos on the glass coffee table of the living room and margaritas in their massive glasses. Taj was looking forward to a night of not talking to Malcolm and making him feel like she was present enough for him. All she wanted to do was just enjoy herself without a care in the world.

It was moments like this that she needed. Moments like this that Maria loved being a part of it with her. Maria's goal was to make sure that Taj had more of these moments. Her healing process had been delayed with keeping everything internalized, but Maria knew that the more she had other things to be happy about, she would get over it all.

Taj plowed her hair out of her face and peeked over at

Maria, who recently grew silent as she pecked away on her phone. Instead of hounding her with questions, Taj smirked softly to herself, took a long sip of her drink and thought about how she was going to sleep without being bothered with Malcolm wanting to spoon and caress her skin while she slept.

She curled her lip with irritation thinking about it. A shiver went down her spine. She could live without him and his need to be in her presence all the time. But Senior claimed that being with him was good for her. Malcolm's presence was what he wanted around Taj. It was always what he wanted for Taj. It irritated the fuck out of her that he continued to dictate what she could do and not do as an adult. But she complied because she didn't want to upset him. She still wanted to be Senior's little girl that was the apple of his eye. She didn't want to taint their relationship because they were all that they had.

Maria let a sigh escape her lips before shoving her phone in Taj's face. "Look, look...I can't believe men still talk like this."

Taj drew her head back to adjust her eyes to the brightness of the screen. Retrieving the phone from Maria's hand, Taj started to scroll through the conversation Maria was having with Tony. Tony was a guy they met the first night they went out. The way Tony approached them was smooth as hell and Taj nudged Maria until she gave in and they exchanged numbers. Maria needed something of her own besides checking on Taj all the time. Taj damn near bullied her into finding something to call her own. From what Taj could tell, he was passionate about life and love and intellectual. Those were things that were crucial in a man, at least to her. Men who cared about the value of life and loving a woman and could think on their own was beautiful to them. Taj even creaked reading through a bit of their conversation.

"Well, shit."

"Exactly. We went out the other night and he was such a gentleman," Maria gushed.

"You should say thank you, Taj." She smirked and cut her eyes at Maria. "You would have given him the cold shoulder and walked away."

"Because I had enough fuck boys to be skeptical," Maria replied.

Although Taj was just as skeptical as Maria was, she didn't feel like this was a situation where she had to rain on the moment and bring up the what if's. Maria was more than capable of weeding through the fuck boys on her own and had done a great job. She had a lot more experience in that area than Taj did. As long as Maria was happy, so was Taj.

Taj smiled softly and handed Maria her phone back.

"We all are. He seems really nice, Maria, and Lord knows you need nice."

"Taj Ali, are you insinuating that I don't like nice?" Maria placed her hand on her chest as though Taj offended her.

Taj let a hearty laugh escape her mouth as she dropped her head back into the cushions of the couch. "Yes, I am. You like that type that has more issues than Cosmopolitan and baby momma drama. So you need nice. Don't run him off."

"I plan to keep him around...well until you know, he starts acting up. Speaking of running men off, what's on going with you and Malcolm? It's been how many years now? What are you doing with him?" Maria had now placed her phone down and turned all her attention to Taj with an eyebrow hiked.

Just because, Taj thought to herself. *I need someone around.*

Instead of letting her thoughts escape her lips, she shrugged. "I don't know. Maybe I'm hoping one day it will just click and I'll open up to him and let that shit flow."

Maria tilted her head to the side and pushed her brow together. "No."

Taj mirrored her expression and buzzed through clenched teeth. "Say it."

With a heavy sigh, Maria sat up off the cushions and turned her body to face Taj fully.

"Well, for one, I know you barely like him and you damn sure don't love him. So, why even keep him strung along?"

Taj didn't want to respond, but Maria's bright eyes were demanding an answer from her. A truthful answer. "Because, I need to feel something. Even if it's not as intense as I want it to be, it's still something..."

"You still love *him*, don't you?"

Taj sighed lightly, licked her lips, and plowed her hands through her hair again. Her eyes clenched close and slightly shook her head. Maria didn't need her to answer, the reaction was enough. But Taj still replied.

"Yes. With every piece of my soul. Because I can't have him. Maybe I'm broken, but I cannot shake Indigo's imprint off me. You ever feel like you can still feel them?"

Maria nodded and then let a light laugh fill the space between them. "He put some good shit on you, girl. Any man coming behind that is going to have a hell of time. Even four years later, your yoni is still feigning for him."

Taj laid her head into the cushions and curled her body up. "That shit was magic. Like feel it all over my body, broken yoni good. Irreplaceable, good. Tattooed on my soul, can never erase him, *good*."

"Look at you mourning over the dick," Maria teased, smacking her lips and lighting the mood. "Mourned for years for the dick."

A lighthearted laugh left Taj's lips and she droned in the memory of Indie.

"No, that was a bonus. I've been mourning for four years and I really should get a grip on this. I really should be over it.

But there's a light, an energy that I will never be able to touch or submerge myself in again. That's what I'm mourning over. That's what I miss. Everything that was him."

"Whew chile," Maria huffed, falling back into the cushions. "That's some heavy shit."

"It is but..." Taj trailed off into her own world of Indigo again. "But I have to stop this obsession of what was and what could have been. I haven't been living life. I've been stuck in this haze, trying to hold on to him. Trying to hold on to Bubba. But all I can do is hold them in my heart and move on. I've got to move on."

Maria placed her hand on top of Taj's that rested on her thigh. A gentle brush of the thumb across her knuckle from Maria was silent assurance. "You got this."

꧁ 5 ꧂

A jai Carter

WITH KINGSTON in one arm and the baby bag in the other, Ajai struggled to put her key in the door and let herself in. Kingston was almost two and refused to walk if she were anywhere around. She appreciated being wanted by her baby boy, but right now, it was more annoying than it was adorable. Finally, after a few minutes of struggling to juggle him, the keys and the baby bag, she unlocked the door and forcefully pushed it open.

"You know, had you just gotten down, we would've been here to see you a lot sooner," She muttered her agitation under her breath. She stepped in and heard footsteps get closer. Startled slightly, she looked up to see Indigo. Immediately, all her agitation dropped from her face and a smile took over.

Ajai excitedly dropped the baby bag off her shoulder and

onto the floor before she clashed into Indigo's body and hugged him as tight as she could with her free arm.

"What are you doing here?"

Wrapping both of his arms around them, Indie chuckled lightly. "You must've missed me because you've never been this happy to see me."

"Absence makes the heart grow fonder and you've missed so much," she gushed, letting him go to step back and look him over. The last time Ajai saw Indie he was clinging to life in a hospital bed. After the second attempt of reviving him, she was sure he was gone. She was unable to stomach his mother's wales or Ricky's frantic pleads anymore.

She pushed that night in the back of her mind, but now that her eyes were on him, the moments flashed back for a moment. She hated ever telling Senior that he didn't make it so prematurely. Things would have been different if she hadn't, but she couldn't go back in time to change anything. He was here, smiling, breathing and walking on his own.

"You haven't met Bleu yet, have you?" Her smile was still plastered on her face as she flashed her eyes from Indie to Bleu. "Say hi, Bleu..."

Bleu shyly buried his face into Ajai's shoulder after Indie flashed a warm smile at him. "I guess that's my fault, cuh. I ain't been around, but you'll get used to me."

"Hmm," Ajai hummed after kicking the door closed and traveling into the living room to put Bleu down on his mat to play with his blocks.

"Are you staying around or are you going to disappear on us again?"

Indie let a sigh escape his lips. "Honestly, I wasn't even planning on coming back here."

Ajai peered up and him and her head shook before she took a seat on the couch. "You know you were a light for a lot of people. And when you left, it's like that light left, too. I don't even see it in you anymore."

Indie propped himself up on the wall that separated the living room from the entrance of the small house. With a scratch of his beard, he let his hum rumble against his teeth and let his shoulders drop. He felt different. Four years changed him and it wasn't for the better, either. "Can I be honest?"

"When have you ever been anything but?" Ajai returned his question with a question and her arms folded over her chest.

"I feel stagnant ...and stuck. Like I did nothing these past four years but float through it." His admission made his head hang, which was rare for him. Ajai was more of a sister than a friend, and whatever doubts or fears he had would stay safe with her.

"What's going on with you, Indie? Why are you back here? Ain't nothing here for you but trouble." She trailed off into her own thoughts which made Indie lift his head and look at her. She looked down at her hands and twirled her thumbs around each other. "What did Ricky tell you to get you back here?"

"That Joey was in some trouble. You know something I don't? Seems like everyone does," he mumbled it, but Ajai heard him loud and clear.

She couldn't bring herself to say anything to him about everything happening in the hood. Instead, she cleared her throat and said, "I don't know if I should get attached to you again. Especially, if you're leaving soon."

"I'm not leaving until I find out what the fuck has been going on. Y'all so tight lipped about shit." He grew irritated with the circles this conversation was doing. He just wanted someone to tell him something. Ajai had never been the one to keep him out of the loop. She heard and saw everything, so why she was being so secretive was driving him up a wall.

Ajai studied him, still going back and forth with herself about whether she was going to tell him what she'd heard Ricky whispering about. She wasn't even supposed to know what the streets were saying. Since she had Bleu, Ricky had done the best he could at protecting them and separating her connection with the block.

"I mean, it's been hell around here enough with you gone. It was damn near an uprising when you left. Your being here just makes everything shaky."

Indie grunted and nodded slowly. "I'm a threat?"

Ajai broke eye contact and licked her dry lips and ran her hand over her jeans.

"Indie, we thought we lost you once. I don't want to go through that again. I don't want to see Ricky trying to deal with that again. My suggestion is that you do what you have to do for Joey and get ghost again."

"Ajai, this talking in code shit is about to piss me off. Just tell me what's up." Indie demanded. "Why do all you refuse to say what's up? That shit is irritating as fuck."

"You're not a threat, Indie, you're a target. And that target is on the back of your head."

Ajai let her words linger in the air. She pushed herself off the couch, went to scoop Bleu up in her arms and headed into the bedroom. She was happy to see him. Everyone was happy to see him, but Indie was a constant reminder of what she thought had died down. Niggas in the hood weren't about to let him come back and pick up his life where he left it. They all thought that he was dead and she honestly felt that it would have been better that way. But now that he was back, it was a matter of time before word got out and people started looking for him again.

❧ 6 ❧

I ndie

JOEY AND AJAI had both successfully gotten into his head and made it spin. Indie roamed from the kitchen to the backyard to smoke and back inside of the house until Ricky got home. Every so often, he would mutter *target* to himself. Someone needed to tell him the truth about what was happening in the hood, and Ricky was going to be the person to tell him. He hadn't been home for a full week yet and he was already fed up with the bullshit and secrecy. He was now second guessing coming back home.

As Ricky turned the doorknob to enter the house, Indie glanced down at the screen of his phone before turning the TV off.

"You must be used to sitting in the dark."

Ricky stumbled over the baby bag by the front door as he

reached for the light switch. Closing the door behind him, he secured it and looked at Indie staring into space.

"Ay, nigga, you good?"

Indie didn't answer. He didn't even move like he heard what Ricky asked him. He was so consumed with the little bit of information that Joey and Ajai gave him that he was starting to over think. The weed didn't help the situation, either. He thought that it would calm his thoughts, but all it did was amplify everything.

Ricky raised his brow and studied him. Just as he was about to open his mouth and ask, *nigga what the fuck is up?* Indie snapped back to reality and looked at him.

"Why did you really call me back here?"

Ricky squinted his eyes and Indie spoke up again. "Don't bullshit me, nigga. I know something is going on. None of this shit feels right. The second I came back here, everything felt off. You, Joey, even Ajai ain't right. It's like I'm in a fucking alternate universe. Everyone looks the same, talks the same, but the way y'all are moving is makin' me real skeptical. And you know I look at everyone like this, but you tell somethin'."

"Nigga," Ricky groaned.

"Nah, don't. Fuck is up, nigga? If it's love, keep it one hundred with me."

Ricky scratched his head, groaned and stalked over to the back door. Throwing his head over to the door, Indie nodded at Ricky and stood up. Once they were outside in the night air, Ricky pulled a blunt from his pocket and sparked it. After a few drafts, he passed it over to Indie.

Blowing the smoke into the air, Indie cut his eyes over to Ricky and said, "I've decided to stay. I can't run from this shit anymore. It doesn't even feel like home no more out here. Something is going on. You either going to tell me or I'm going to put my ear to the streets and find out myself."

Ricky chuckled and turned to face Indie fully. "Nigga, why you so hellbent on this shit?"

"What you mean *why*? Nigga, you ain't keeping it straight with me and I got a fucking problem with that. You tell me I need to get here, and I shut down everything I had going on to get here, and y'all playing with a nigga like I ain't fuckin' bright or some shit."

"Oh, you bright," Ricky joked, but Indie wasn't in the mood to play around. He wore it on his face. "Aight man."

Indie hiked his shoulders and shot Ricky a look of agitation that could slice the air. "Ricky. Stop fucking with me."

"Nigga, word on the street that there was a price on your head. Them niggas set you up. And when TK got word that you were set up, he put an order out for peace. He didn't want no more bloodshed," Ricky finally admitted to Indie.

Indie's hiked shoulders dropped and a heavy groan escaped his lips, Ricky could feel the heaviness that instantly invaded Indie's spirit. Indie ran his hand over his head and grunted at the news he was processing. "Any word on who?"

Ricky shook his head. Indie nodded his head like he was accepting the answer and was okay with the news, but he was doing anything but. It was unsettling and it bothered every part of his being. "Ain't no word on who."

Ricky scratched the stubble of his facial hair and shook his head. "Nah."

"And it was just my head?" Indie had to repeat the question over in his head and out loud. "Not you? Not Joey?"

"Just yours."

"Does Joey know about this?"

Ricky shrugged. "I have no idea. Like I said, the little nigga been pulled away from me and TK. Stopped slangin' to run missions and shit."

"Aight," Indie murmured into the night air.

Ricky stood by his side and smoked the blunt while Indie consumed himself with his thoughts again. Trying to put the pieces of the puzzle together that he had, his calmness was battling with his irritation to take over the situation. He wanted peace, but he wasn't going to get that until he sifted through the chaos that surrounded him. The chaos that he tried to escape from for years.

He must have stood there silently with his thoughts roaring for almost ten minutes before he consciously remembered to inhale and exhale.

"I want to meet with TK. Make that shit happen."

Ricky was in the middle of inhaling smoke from the blunt and choked hearing Indie's request. "Nigga what? You done with the game, remember?"

Indie wasn't here for Ricky being the comedian of the hour. "You know good and damn well I wasn't. Fuck you think kept me floatin' in Oakland?"

"Your good looks and your charm." Ricky chuckled with a shrug that caused Indie to suck his teeth and cut his eyes.

"Fuck you, nigga. I need that meeting. I need to get back in with him. One of these niggas know somethin' and I'm going to find that shit out."

Ricky reluctantly huffed and gave in to the demand. "Okay."

"I can't fuckin' lie, I feel really uneasy about niggas wanting to take me out when my girl was in the car. I'll find out who the fuck was behind that shit and ain't no talkin' when I do. You ridin' or nah?"

Ricky pursed his lips and cut a *nigga really* look at Indie. "You think I'm going to let you see some action without me?"

"I don't know. You're a family man now. You turnin' soft and shit."

"As long as I get home and they're good, it's good."

"Tomorrow, make that meeting happen."

UNTITLED

I'm an urban legend, South Central in a certain section
Can't express how I curbed detectives
Guess it's evidence of a divine presence
Blessings, help me out at times I seem reckless

- Nipsey Hussle: Victory Lap

R icky Adams

"You know what you're going to tell that nigga when you walk in here?" Ricky looked over his shoulder at Indie sitting in the passenger seat. "I know you got a plan."

They crept down the street toward TK's spot and Ricky needed to know what the game plan was before he walked in there with a resurrected Indigo. Indie was silent, making Ricky worry. The last thing he wanted was to walk into TK's spot with a dumbass look on his face and guess what the next move would be.

"C'mon, nigga know you got to be thinkin' something. You used to be the brains of the operation, now you just here looking stupid."

Indigo sucked his teeth. "I just want to talk to the nigga about who shot me, that's it."

"You think he knows?" Ricky asked with a brow raised.

Indigo pressed his lips together and cut his eye at him. "Aight, you got a point."

"Tell me what happens in this hood that TK don't know about?" Indigo went on. "Somebody knows something."

Ricky looked at him oddly and let his head tilt. "So, you want revenge?"

Indigo rumbled with laughter before he slid his hand down his face and exhaled in amusement. "Nah, not really. Those niggas snuck up on me. If you going to take me out, let me see that shit comin'. I've never been the type of nigga to run from nothin'. You want to take me out, take me out because it ain't hard."

"Thunder Cat, you got about nine lives." Ricky couldn't help the smirk that crossed his face as a light bulb went off in his head. He was happy to know that Indie was still with the shit when it came down to making sure these niggas knew who they were dealing with. He was also concerned that this had turned Indie cold to everything and everyone.

"I know you got a way in to find out who ordered that hit."

"I figured I'll get in with TK and go from there. I wanted to get the hell out the game, but life had different plans. Might as well go for it. What do I have to lose at this point?" Indigo muttered before speaking up. "I've taken so many L's. What's another one. But if this is a win, you know this is going to be the last time we do this shit, right? We don't have time to waste no more. It's all or nothing."

"Even though I've heard that before, that's that fucking energy I've been missing. Let's get to the money and get the fuck out." Ricky grinned and stopped his car on the curb in front of TK's spot.

Indie surveyed the area and got himself together before pulling his hoodie off his head and stepping out so everyone could see that he was alive and he was back. He was sure that his presence would cause everyone to tense up and question why he decided to show up now. Ricky stepped out of the car and looked around at the crowd in front of the house, staring at Indie with questions swirling around. Looking over his shoulder, Ricky smirked and threw his head toward the door.

Ricky and Indie walked up the sidewalk to the door with tiny smirks on their faces as a few of the niggas started to whisper like bitches.

"That's that nigga, Indigo."

"I thought he was dead."

"That nigga been alive this whole time."

"Ain't this some shit..."

Indigo ignored the whispers and maneuvered through the crowd of people looking at him with wide eyes and disbelief etched on their faces. They made it inside after getting patted down. Ricky looked at TK's reaction after laying his eyes on Indigo. Initially, TK sat in his seat and stared at Indigo, almost like he was seeing something. The energy surrounding TK was off. Almost like he couldn't believe that Indie had the balls to show up after years, but amused that he did. TK was stuck for a bit until Indie shifted his weight and let a crooked smile cross his face. TK pushed his brows together.

"You goin' to look at me like I'm a ghost, nigga?" Indie chuckled a bit. "Or are you gon' say some shit?"

Ricky smirked, realizing how cool Indie was playing this meeting. Compared to his irritation the night before, Indie was as calm as he would get. He was levelheaded enough to play a game with TK and not have him question his motive.

TK rose to his feet and walked around his desk and walked over to Indie. After sizing him up and studying him closely, he greeted Indie with a handshake and a half hug.

"Nigga, we thought you were dead. Went to the fuckin' funeral and everything. What the fuck, nigga?"

Indie smirked and stepped back. "You know how shit goes. The hood was hot. I had to lay low for a minute. But I'm back. What the fuck is goin' on around here?"

"Ain't shit but the same shit. What you need, nigga? Say that word, I got you. Shit, you real," TK blew with an unreadable expression on his face.

Indie shifted his eyes over to Ricky. He felt something was off with TK. "Man I don't need shit but some work."

"Oh bet." TK nodded and responded anxiously. Indie rose his brow, watching how nervous TK got after he stepped back. "I got you, nigga, I got you. You know what we need to do first, though? Welcome you back from the dead. Nigga, you rose like your fuckin' Lazarus."

Indie shook his head. "That ain't necessary, man. I just came here for some work. Ain't no need to—"

"You always been a humble nigga. Ain't too many niggas that come back from that shit. You got to tell me how you managed that." TK continued to press the issue.

Indie tried his best to keep his face from showing how bothered he was with TK's need to go overboard with his return home. The only niggas who were interested in doing shit like this were niggas with a guilty conscious that were looking to redeem themselves to people who didn't know they ever did anything. "TK."

"I ain't taking no. Rico! Go put the word out, Indie is back home! Tell the set to come out and welcome this nigga home! Show Azul some fuckin' love."

TK threw his arm over Indie's shoulder and Ricky shook his head at Indie's unenthused expression. Indie was bothered by all of it, but if this led him to an answer he was looking for, then so be it.

Irritation didn't even cover what Indie was feeling. He was standing in the corner of the house, holding a drink in his hand that one of TK's girls poured for him. He refused to drink it, though. His paranoia was even higher than it had ever been. He refused to drink or eat anything he didn't see made. He held the cup and looked around the party at everyone. The faces were familiar, just tired and pain settled into the creases, but they still found joy in the smallest things. A few niggas from the neighborhood approached him.

Exchanging a handshake, the shorter of the two looked up at Indie with a crooked smirk. "How's your heart, young nigga?"

Indie nodded, not keeping his eyes off of the crowd of people and still engaged with him. "It's good. I'm cool."

"It's all love. We been keeping our eyes open from them shooters. We've been chasing a ghost for years, though. Just know we got you. The set love you and we proud, nigga."

Indie welcomed the love and gave each of them a half hug, half handshake and stepped back. "Appreciate it."

"Hold your head."

A few more exchanges were made between a few more people and Indie. He would smile and nod in appreciation and thankfulness of their expression. He made sure he remembered their faces. He shifted his eyes from the people walking past him to a guy TK was talking to in the corner almost out of the sight of everyone. Indie's height allowed him to see more than everyone else could. With a nudge to Ricky's shoulder, Indie slightly turned his body toward Ricky.

"Who is the nigga talking to TK? He looks familiar. I've seen him before. Ain't he from a block over?"

Ricky glanced over the rim of his cup and spoke. "Fuck if I know, but he does look like we had a run in before."

Indie couldn't let the opportunity to be a smartass pass. "Who haven't you had run ins with? Gotdamn Rambo."

"Fuck you. I grew up. Now I ask a question before I start shootin'."

Indie laughed and looked around this party TK threw for him and curled his lip in disgust of the shenanigans. The girls were loose and anyone that hadn't approached him were huddled up together, giving the girls the attention they sought after. Everyone in his eyes was a snake, including TK. He was going to get to the bottom of it, and when he did, the hood wouldn't be the same when he was done. He wasn't playing the get back game. He didn't have time for shit like that. What he had was an insatiable need to make shit right.

"Bleu calmed you down like that?" Indie asked, spotting Monica. His lip curled even more and he dropped his head. "Who the fuck ran through her?"

"Everyone," Ricky spoke up with a disgusted tone. "She been sucking and fucking for free. Don't dive back into that shit. You're going to come out burning with a kid you don't want. She got like two damn kids."

"Damn," Indie blew, slowly side stepping to the exit. There was no need to run. Monica was closing in on him and he didn't want to draw any attention to himself. He planted his feet and prepared himself to shut her down.

Monica had gained weight in all the wrong places. Her face looked tired and discolored, but Indie could understand two kids in a four-year span could do a number on a woman's body. It wasn't too much her size that threw him for a loop, it was her outfit that was about two sizes too small for her new body and the loud smell of her perfume to cover up whatever body funk she had going.

"Damn, Indie, been a while."

Nodding, he replied. "Yeah, long time. You been good?"

"Yeah, where's your girl? You know that one you curved me for with the bushy hair?" She let a smug ass smirk cross her lips and Indie rolled his eyes at the comment. He'd done a great job not thinking about Taj, but now that Monica had brought it up, he had the itch again.

"Good, I guess," Indie answered. "Look, we got some shit to do. We'll see you around."

Indie caught Ricky's eyes and threw his head toward the exit. "You take care of yourself, aight?"

"Yeah, you too," Monica said, watching Indie walk off.

When Ricky and Indie got outside, Ricky looked over to him and asked. "Where we going?"

"I don't fuckin' care, I just needed to get out of there."

🙣 8 🙢

A jai

"Sнннн," Ajai hushed Bleu, bouncing him on her hip as she tiredly stalked to the kitchen to grab him a cup of juice to get him to stop whining. She silently cussed to herself for not getting it before they fell asleep in the bed.

"Ju..ju..ju..ju," Bleu whined over and over and over again, forcing Ajai to roll her eyes and quicken her step to the kitchen. "Mama...ju!"

"Boy, I heard you the first twenty-five times," she answered, reaching the fridge and pulling it open to retrieve a cup of juice she poured before she climbed into the bed. Handing him the juice, Bleu snatched it and started to sip away and rest his head on her shoulder.

Plopping down on the couch, she laid her head on the cushion and bounced him until he drifted back to sleep. "Lucky little ass. I'm going to be up all night now."

Turning the TV on, she laid him down by her and grabbed a blanket off the back of the couch and covered him up. Ajai tucked her legs underneath her butt and watched whatever was playing on the screen. It didn't matter what it was, as long as it put her to sleep.

Just as she got comfortable, Indie eased into the house, trying his best not to startle anyone. Closing the door behind him, he looked up and spotted her staring at the screen. His eyes went from her to Bleu, snoring lightly. "Y'all good?"

Ajai nodded. "He was whining for juice and now I'm awake just thinking. You good?"

Indie shrugged and rubbed the back of his neck. "Shit, as good as it gets."

"Your running for TK again? Ain't that the opposite of what you were pioneering against in the first place? There's a difference between being a gang banger and a gang member." Ajai pressed her lips together while her eyes flashed a hint of disappoint toward him.

They stared at each other for a brief moment before she opened her mouth again. "Indie, what are you doing? This is not why you were given a second chance."

He scoffed lightly, rolling his eyes at Ajai's comment. "I'm standing here, what you mean?"

"Nigga, you know what I mean." Ajai smacked her lips and rolled her eyes just as hard as he did. "Where your dreams at? Where your goals at? I've been around this gang shit all my life and I've barely seen a few niggas make it past thirty. But never in my life have I ever seen a nigga make it after being shot that many times. You need to make sure that what you are doing right now isn't what you're going to be doing forever."

Indie sat on the other couch and ran his hand down his tired face. "You're right. You're absolutely right. Ajai, trust me,

I got a plan and it has no choice but to go right. I don't have a plan B. Ricky ain't going to be gang bangin' forever, either."

"I pray not. He's getting deeper and deeper into this shit, Indie. I'm not trying to be a single mother because of this gang shit," Ajai released with a heavy sigh and she grew quiet. She finally said her fears out loud and the sound of it against her ears made her breathing hitch.

"A dollar for your thoughts." Indie coaxed her to say what was on her mind.

She sighed and looked up at the ceiling. "I should have had my own salon by now. I just kept pushing it off and then I got pregnant and now all that I want, and need is a reach."

"You told Ricky what you needed from him?"

Ajai shook her head. "It's not that big. I should be used to it."

"If it's big to you, it's big. And you never need to get used to this shit," Indie spoke up. "Ricky is you and you are him. Y'all need to be real with each other and put that shit on the table. Keep it all the way one hundred."

"Look at you giving me game like a big brother." She chuckled, looking over at Indie. "Thank you, but now I need to give you some."

"Here we go. What did I do now?"

"It's what you didn't do. You have been here for a week and haven't even seen your momma. You know you're foul for that shit. Everything she's done and dealt with for your yellow ass. Nigga, you better go see your momma. Ricky goes and checks in to make sure she has everything she needs, but Ricky ain't you."

Indigo dropped his head and hummed. He didn't know why he was putting off seeing his mother. Maybe it was because he didn't want to see the look on her face when she looked at him. He didn't want to answer the millions of questions she wanted answered, but she deserved answers.

"You right," he hummed.

"Oh wait, what you say?" Ajai asked, moving her hair from over her ear. "Say that again, I didn't hear you. The TV was too loud."

Indigo snickered. "You got the volume on like five. You heard me the first time I said it. Quit playing."

"Appease me, bro, and say it again."

"Aight." He pushed himself off the couch and started walking toward his room. "You right. You got it."

"You better handle that shit. How about that?"

"I hear you!"

9

I ndie

FALLING BACK ON THE BED, Indigo stared at the ceiling. There was still a raging war in him and he would give anything for it to stop, even if it were for a moment. He tried everything to stop, but there was only one touch, one voice, one light that would settle the war.

Taj.

Whatever power Taj possessed, it made him calm. Just the thought of her touch would calm him. But not anymore. The thought of her wasn't doing it for him. He needed to touch her, smell the scent of her skin, put his nose in her hair, and become one with her again.

He shook the thought of her away and sat up on the edge of the bed. He pulled his shirt over his head and tossed it into the pile of dirty clothes. Standing up and stepping out his pants, he sat back down and grabbed his phone.

Indie hit Joey's name on the screen of his phone and waited while it rang. He just wanted to make sure everything was okay. Their conversation played over in his mind and he wanted to revisit it. After the fourth ring, Joey picked up.

"What you want, nigga?" Joey grunted. "Fuck you callin' me for?"

"Nigga, you better take that bass out your throat before I knock it out," Indie threatened and then he smiled. "Fuck you got going on?"

Joey blew heavy and chuckled lightly. "Ain't shit, when you coming to see Ma?"

"Tomorrow. You gon' be around?"

"Yeah, I might be. You good?"

Indie wasn't going to alarm Joey that he wasn't good. "Yeah, I'm cool. Just checking on you. I'll see you tomorrow."

"Aight," Joey replied before ending their call.

Laying back on the bed, Indie started scrolling through pictures of Taj on his phone. His heart ached, but he continued to ignore it. But it was getting to the point where he couldn't ignore the ache. He couldn't be here without her. Especially, after seeing Monica and how she fell off. He knew he dodged a bullet and found a diamond in Taj. He wanted that diamond back, but it would have to wait until the time was right. He didn't even know when that would be, but assumed he would find out when the atmosphere shifted. He had other pressing issues that he hoped and prayed that weren't going to draw themselves out. For his peace and sanity, he needed it.

UNTITLED

All I got is these broken clocks
I ain't got no time
Just burnin' daylight
Still love, and it's still love, and it's still love
Nothin' but love for you

- SZA: Broken Clocks

10

T aj

"Oh shit!" Taj squealed with fear, feeling Malcolm's cold hands pressed against her bare waist. The unwelcoming chill it sent through her body made her jump out of her skin and pull away from him. Forcing a regretful smile on her face, she looked at him standing in their kitchen with his duffle bag hanging off his shoulder and his suitcase parked by the front door. She instantly started regretting wearing a sports bra and a pair of short shorts around her own house. Malcolm looked at her with a burning lust in his eyes, and it provoked her skin to crawl. Sex was always had on her terms, and right now, her terms were to withdraw from him as much as she could.

She analyzed both him and his things and tried to figure out how she didn't hear him come through the door. For the last week, she was able to get work done and enjoy the time she had to herself while Malcolm was away on his business trip. It was wrong to look forward to the times he went out of town and dread the moments when he returned, but she found herself doing it time after time.

"I didn't mean to scare you," Malcolm apologized, taking a step toward Taj. For every step he took to get closer to her, she took a step back. Although Malcolm didn't mind being the aggressor in the relationship, this dance was a subliminal message of the status of their relationship.

Every time Malcolm tried to open one door, he realized that there was another trap door to keep him out. But still, he loved Taj and he even started thinking about spending the rest of his life with her. She was guarded, but he was sure with the proper love and care that he would be able to break down those walls that she built around her, her heart and spirit.

Taj pulled her bottom lip between her teeth and cleared her throat.

"It's okay, really. I just thought that you were still out of town for another day."

"I came back early. I missed you, Ali." Malcolm grabbed her waist and pulled her into him with a force that made her uncomfortable. Attempting to cover her mouth with his, Taj pulled away from him, but his grip tightened. "We don't connect like this anymore. I miss feeling you. Being with you. Hearing you sing my name."

"Malcolm," Taj grunted, trying to get out of his grip. "Stop, I have work to do."

"Fuck that work. You haven't given me none of that good loving in months," he said, pushing his lips into her. The taste of gin coated her lips. She wasn't going to win this battle. When Malcolm was drunk, he got far more aggressive than she liked. And if he didn't get his way, it was going to be a long night for her. She wasn't in the mood to be up all night, arguing about why she didn't want him to touch her.

"You've been drinking." She tried to get away from him again, but his grip got tighter and he slammed her into a wall. Hard enough that she got the picture, but it didn't do any damage to her body. "Let's do this later."

His lips found their way to her neck and he interlocked his fingers in hers. She was pinned between his body and the wall. Sloppy kisses were placed on her and it made her stomach turn, threatening to spill its contents if he didn't stop. After all this time, he still didn't know how she liked to be touched or handled.

Indie would have never handled me like this...

Fighting Malcolm wouldn't work. He was stronger than her, and the liquor gave him more strength to hold her still and get what he wanted. The worst feeling Malcolm invoked in her spirit was vulnerability. She didn't feel protected. She didn't feel valued. She felt like a piece of meat. She felt like he loved her for what she could offer and not who she truly was.

Malcolm hungrily attacked her flesh with his lips and his intoxicated tongue. Taj had to talk herself down and relax.

It'll be over soon.

Just relax, it won't be that bad.

Baby, just keep your eyes closed.

She gave into him and let him have his away. She counted down the moment until it was over. His grunts, his sweat dripping from his chin, and his hasty strokes made her stare at the clock on the wall slowly tick away until it was over. Taj had really settled into a fuck it attitude. If this was the only love she was going to get, then fuck it. She'd rather be alone.

"Oh yeah, baby," he groaned, pounding into her like he was giving her the best sex ever. But if he only knew, it wasn't doing a thing but wasting her time and making her heart harder toward him. "You got some bomb ass pussy."

Taj squeezed her eyes shut until it was finally over. Closing her eyes and letting her mind roam off to everything but this awful round of sex. The only thing her mind seemed to think about was that she had rarely had great sex with Malcolm. If anything, it was enough to do the trick, but it was never...spine tingling...orgasmic...can't walk right for a few days. Malcolm grunted after pulling himself out and smacking her on the ass. Taj didn't even bother to look back at him. She adjusted her bra and pulled her shorts up, gathered her phone and her laptop and disappeared into the guest room. Locking the door behind her, she hurried to the bathroom to wash his drunken scent off of her.

She sat on the floor of the shower with her knees drawn into her chest and her cheek pressed against her knees. The hot water beat against her body, saturating her curls and washing the tears from her face. The overwhelming feeling of being unprotected took over her. She figured that Malcolm had passed out because he didn't try to come and cuddle with her like he would normally do. He could stay on the other side of the condo; she was fine with that. She wasn't ready to see him or talk to him after what just took place. Although she felt anger and pain and everything else involved with those emotions, she was relieved that she opted into getting on birth control. She couldn't risk being unhappy and being unhappy with a child from him.

Morning came and Taj was dressed and packing up her things for a day of meetings at the office. She zipped around the living room, collecting her papers. Stuffing her briefcase with everything she needed, Taj grabbed a cup of tea and Malcolm eased out of their bedroom.

"Ali." The sound of his voice automatically made her anxiety shoot up through the roof. It had already been high most of the night, so she didn't get much sleep. Now she was anxious and annoyed.

She looked over her shoulder at him and picked up her phone. "Not now Malcolm, I'm late."

"Give me a second, babe. Please, just a second," Malcolm practically pleaded. "Let me just talk to you for a second."

With a huff, she turned around to face him and placed her palms against the countertop. "What do you want?"

"I want to say I'm sorry about last night," he spoke up, standing on the other side of the counter, staring at her, but she broke eye contact. "I was out of line. I had too many drinks on the flight. I shouldn't have handled you like that. Let me make it up to you."

"Malcolm, right now I have to get to work. We'll circle back around to this later," she replied, recollecting all of her things and walking toward the door.

He trailed her. "Ali, I don't want you to go to work like this."

Refusing to look at him, she placed her hand on the steel doorknob and thought about firing back a smart comment, but instead, she chuckled to herself and scoffed softly and replied. "I go to work like this every day."

She left him there to stew in his shame of his behavior that she tolerated. They were equally as guilty. Malcolm was out of line; he knew it, and Taj was emotionally unavailable to him. It was a toxic situation they created and lived in. The time to end this was weighing heavily on Taj's spirit. She just had to figure out how she was going to cut the cord that had grown between the two of them.

Taj arrived at the office, parked her car, inhaled, glanced

down at the tattoo on her wrist and dropped her head back. Closing her eyes, she exhaled and released everything. Well, tried to release everything. Once she traveled inside the building, she picked up a couple of reports off of Maria's desk and whisked into her office. After kicking the door shut with her foot, Taj plopped down in her chair. She pushed her hands through her hair, scratched her scalp, and groaned in frustration. Frustration that she felt like *this*, frustration that *this* was her reality and ultimately frustrated that she decided to stay in some weird shit like *this*.

"Taj, what are you in here pouting over?" Maria questioned, opening the door and walking into her office, closing the door behind her.

Taj glanced up at Maria and debated on whether or not she was going to mention Malcom's assertiveness the night before. But that would only cause Maria to pull out the razor blades and the lemon juice. Deciding against it, she huffed and said, "I'm just tired and we need to get the grant so we can get this shit moving. Can we redirect our energy to that?"

Maria nodded and studied Taj's demeanor. Maria could easily pick up on the heaviness around Taj, but she knew how Taj felt about talking about her personal life in the office. But it didn't stop her from saying. "Taj Ali."

Taj looked around the room like she was lost to what Maria possibly had to say to her. "What?"

"You know what it is. I need to know what it is." Maria smacked her lips and folded her arms across her chest. "You walked in here with your brows pinned together and that scowl on your face. So, I know something is up."

Taj inhaled and hummed as she released it and massaged her temples, causing her eyes to roll in the back of her head. "You want to know what's up? This grant. We need to make sure we have everything for that in by the time we go to lunch.

Have everyone refocus and get presentations tidied up, please?"

Maria nodded and walked out of the office to leave Taj alone with her own thoughts. She glanced over at the picture of her and Bubba on the corner of her desk. "It's not on me. All right, Taj, let's get to it. Tighten up."

I ndie

"WHO IS that walking in my house?" Diane called from the kitchen.

Every Sunday, she made dinner like she was expecting an army to show up. It was a habit that she couldn't break, even if she tried. Her Sunday's consisted of church in the morning, tidying up the house, cooking dinner and waiting on Indie to call her and tell her that everything was okay. Up until recently, he hadn't missed a Sunday. She missed him being home. She missed him being around and making sure that everything was taken care of. Especially Joey. Joey needed Indie around, and the four years they spent without him definitely changed them. Diane's spirit wasn't okay without her Indigo. She understood that all of this was for his safety and hers, but she'd had her fill of it. She was over this two weeks after he left four years ago.

There were days where her thoughts were consumed with

the phone call she got that night at work and a week later, lowering an empty casket into the ground just to keep up the appearance. Diane often questioned what if. What if Indigo really lost his life the night? What if Joey loses his? She cleared her head and opened her mouth again to ask. "I said, who is that walking in my house?"

Joey looked back at Indie and smirked a bit.

"Just me, Ma!"

"You staying or you disappearing on me?" She questioned, not moving from her position.

She developed this habit of not looking at Joey until he was headed out the door. She took a snapshot of what he was wearing just in case she got a call in the middle of the night that something happened to him. Although she prayed that she would never get that call again, she knew what kind of life her sons were involved in. It was the same life that she grew up in. This was her normal, but there was nothing normal about it. Every man in her family was affiliated with the set. They lived by the set, they died by the set. It was almost inevitable that her sons would follow in footsteps of the men she was raised by.

Joey chuckled and sat down at the small dining room table and watched her stir the pots and glance at her phone every so often, anticipating Indie's call.

"You know your damn brother hasn't called me in two weeks? What the hell is he doing that he can't call me?"

Joey shrugged his shoulders. "Maybe he's busy, Ma. He be in his own little world like we don't exist."

Indie rolled his eyes at Joey from behind the wall. He examined her frame and her face. Although her voice was lively, her face wasn't. His heart sank, and decided to speak up and say, "Because, Ma, it's better to see you in person."

She froze. Her breathing stopped and her brain tried to process what was reality and what was her imagination. She started walking toward him with tears cradled in her eyes. She wrapped her arms around him tightly. This was probably the tightest she'd ever held on to her oldest. Everything about him felt...different. Diane picked up the change of his natural scent, his energy, and the way he held her back just as secure as she held him. Indie held on to her like he would never hold her again.

Excited to have her son back, Diane accepted that he was different and silently hoped that the son she knew would return. Her heart fluttered with thankfulness and she cried silently into his chest that had buffed up a bit. Indie graced his mother's back with the gentle rubs of his fingers and rested his head on top of hers.

"Stop that cryin', girl," he muttered into her hair, following a soft kiss. "Everything's good."

She was so happy to see him, to touch him, to smell him. Her son was home. After praying that he would be able to come home, here he was, holding on to her tenderly and gladly welcoming her affection that he once hated. Now there was no such thing as too much. Even Joey smiled at that reunion he was witnessing.

"You gotta be hungry," she spoke up, wiping her face and touching his muscular chest. "My little boy ain't little no more."

The last time she held him like this, he had open wounds all over his torso, covered in blood stained bandages. That vision flashed in her head and she looked up at her son. "How long have you been here?"

"A week or two."

She drew her hand back at him and popped him. "A week or two? Boy!"

"Ma." Indie chuckled. "Listen, I had to lay low for a minute. I'm back."

She studied his face, looking for any sign that he was in distress. "Is everything okay?"

Indie and Joey locked eyes for a moment before Indie directed his attention back to his mom and nodded. "Yeah, everything is cool, Ma. Don't worry about none of that. I'm here, I'm back, and I'm hungry. Ajai can cook, but it's nothing like this."

"So, that's where you been? And it's taken you this long to come see me?" Diane questioned, placing her hands on her hips.

Indie chuckled and ran his tongue across his bottom lip. "Yeah, but I had some things to get together before I came here. You know you're my number one. I had to check in before I popped up."

Diane let a soft smile cross her face and quietly replied, "Okay. You don't have to tell me anymore. I know how it goes."

She turned on her heels to go back into the kitchen to fix her boys' food.

While Diane was busy fixing their plates, Indie sat down and looked at Joey. Everything about Joey looked like Indie four years ago. Confident, courageous, and making waves in his own lane. But even so, Indie still didn't feel like this was something for Joey to be tied up in. The game changed him, killed his youth and stole his innocence. Everything Indie witnessed showed on his face. It made his chest tighten with anxiety knowing that there was nothing he could do to get him out, not this time. Joey had to find his own way and make something out of his life he could be proud of. It was going to be a road of ups and downs that were out of Indie's control, but that didn't stop Indie from saying, "Word in the hood is you that nigga now."

"Yeah, so what?" Joey muttered back with a nonchalant shrug on his shoulders. "You need me for somethin'?"

"I do —"

Indie cut his request short as Diane placed their food on the table and smiled at both of her boys before turning to get her plate off the counter.

"I do..."

"You better off findin' the shit out on your own because I don't want shit to do with what you got going on," Joey replied with a wave of the hand.

Joey's attitude was going to have Indie fly off the handle with him, but he restrained himself as much as he could.

"Boy, I should fu—"

"Indigo, who else knows about you being home?" Diane turned around and took her place at the table.

Indie started eating while shooting Joey a dirty look. "Everyone that needs to know, knows."

"You need to see Mary and..." She stopped and sighed. He knew that she felt just as bad as Ricky did about keeping this from Taj. She was the only girl Indie ever spent time with that she liked. It could be a number of reasons why his mother liked her, but overall, it was because of who she was, and you had no choice but to love her. "Taj."

Indie swallowed hard and dropped his head for a moment. With a sharp inhale, he shook the thought of her off.

"She ain't tryin' to see me, Ma. I'm the last nigga she wants to see."

Diane shook her head and hummed.

"I think it's worth a shot. You know she used to call and check on me, but the calls got further apart and then they just stopped. Mary showed me pictures from her graduation. You would never guess what was on her cap."

Indigo Dreamin'

"I don't think she's closed the door on you just yet. She's still holding on after all this time. I'm telling you, that's not someone you want to miss out on. You've lost enough time."

Indie looked at his mother and thought about it. The seed had been planted and it kept growing through the soil, trying to reach the surface. Choosing to ignore it, he pushed it back into the back of his mind.

"She probably moved on, Ma. She ain't checking for me. She got the world at her feet now. She doesn't need to be bothered with me and my shit. I already did enough damage to her."

Diane nodded and silently agreed not to press the issue anymore, but she knew her son, and she saw the change in him when Taj came into the picture. She also knew that no matter how hard he tried to fight it, he could never stay away from her. They were tied together at the soul, and a connection like that was never easily broken.

I ndie

FOR THE FIRST time in years, the mood in the neighborhood was light, joyous even. The music was blasting and there were actual smiles on people's faces. The outpour of happiness that Indie had returned home was overwhelming and it made Ricky drop his scowl, knowing that they genuinely were happy that Indie was back. It was things like this that made him and Indie fall in love with their neighborhood.

Since word got out that Indie was back, everyone was showing love, even niggas that they had run in's with years back were reaching out to tell Indie how much they respected him and they were happy he was back. It was a different energy Indie brought to the hood. It was missed, and so was he, but still, he was skeptical of the outpour. He couldn't help but wonder where all this energy was when he was around the first time. This was the hood he loved being a part of when he was younger, but was this the hood that really loved him back? Indie decided to accept the outpour of love for now but keep his head on a swivel. No one was going to catch him slipping again.

Ricky leaned on the hood of his car as Indie chopped it up with a couple of niggas from around the way. This is why Ricky wanted Indie to come back home, everyone needed him. His calmness and his contagious spirit.

Indie couldn't finish a complete sentence without someone hollering his name from a passing car and throwing up the set.

"We see you, nigga!"

"This shit is crazy," Indie muttered, walking over to Ricky and pushing the money in his pocket. "A nigga gotta damn near die to get some love around this bitch."

"You know niggas love to be a part of a comeback story." Ricky sparked a blunt and got more comfortable on the hood. Their rounds were finished, and they didn't have anything to do for the rest of the day but bullshit around with everyone else. "You don't look like you are feeling all the love."

"How can I? I got a feeling all this love ain't all love. You feel me?" Indie looked forward at his surroundings. "I got a gut feeling like it's smoke and mirrors or some shit."

"I got a feeling that you trippin'" Ricky blew the smoke from his lungs and looked Indie up and down. "Aight, so say it ain't all love. Who would want you gone? I mean, narrow that shit all the way down because like I said, we had run ins with a gang of niggas. They all out here showing you love."

Indie kissed his teeth, leaned on the hood and continued to study all the joyous faces.

"I don't know, but somebody."

For a brief second, he closed his eyes to reset. His chest was tightening again, and his heart rate was increasing after a few deep breaths. He heard Ricky groan in annoyance.

Indie cracked an eye open and spotted Leroy pushing his cart down the street toward them. Leroy was the neighborhood drunk who had a habit of talking out of his head more than anything else. But Indie always made sure Leroy had someone to talk to, and something to eat.

Indie snickered at Ricky's irritation and said, "Why do you treat that nigga like that? All he needs is a job to keep him out of trouble."

"Here this nigga go with this shit," Ricky muttered with a smack of the teeth. "You always lookin' out for his ass. All he's going to do with that money you give him is drink it away."

Indie kissed his teeth and rolled his eyes at Ricky's comment. "And all we do is sell drugs. What is your point?"

"The nigga is annoying as fuck is my point," Ricky continued to complain as Leroy got closer.

"All the nigga wants is somebody to listen to him." Indie pointed out. "Have some compassion, bro."

"Go ahead and listen to him like you do with them kids. I'm not doing it." Ricky grunted.

"What those kids do to you, nigga?" Indigo couldn't help but frown his face at Ricky's comment.

Since he's been back in L.A., he made it a point to spend every Saturday at youth center, playing basketball and showing the kids how to build different computers on the three old computers that they had there. There was no real money flowing into the center and the kids would rather be hanging out on the block because it was more interesting. But Indie's presence piqued their interest and kept them showing up to see what he was talking about.

"Indigo!" Leroy rejoiced, laying his eyes on Indie and sped up his speed from a slow funeral shuffle to a quick wobble. It was three in the afternoon and Leroy's stagger was comical. He was clearly drunk, but Indie could never remember a time that he wasn't drunk or well on his way to getting there. "I knew it! I knew it!"

"Come on Indie, don't pay that nigga no mind. We got shit to do," Ricky grumbled through a could of smoke flowing from his lips as Indie turned around to meet Leroy halfway and shake his hand before pulling him into a hug.

"Nigga, we don't have shit to do but bullshit. Let it go." Indie said.

"What you been up to, nigga?"

"Man nothing, you know the same shit. I knew you didn't die. You like Tupac. I told everyone that you don't die. The real ones never go out easy."

Indie didn't find it hard to believe that no one believed Leroy, especially with the way he was talking to him now with a slight slur in his speech. Every other word was a stutter or a mutter, but Indie had been talking to Leroy since he was a kid. He was used to it. But just because Leroy was a drunk didn't mean that he was completely out of his mind. He just saw some shit, done some shit and felt some shit that forced him to find peace at the bottom of the bottle.

Indie really couldn't blame him, either. For two years, he spent most of his days drinking and smoking the physical and emotional pain away. There were times where he wanted to slip back into that guy. He was feeling hopeless and lost about everything. In a blink of an eye, he almost lost everything. That hurt him more than he would ever let on. It was more than just having to leave a place he called home, and a woman he found himself connected to on a whole other level. It was the mourning of losing who he was. He couldn't figure out how he was going to get back to himself, but being here was a start.

Indie smirked and studied Leroy. "You good? You need

something to eat? A ride or something? When is the last time you ate?"

"Nah, I ate earlier," Leroy declined, studying Indie in return. "TK put you back to work, huh? I always said you were loyal. Come back and work for him."

Indie squinted his eyes. Usually, between him and Ricky, they would talk to him just to pass time. Every so often, Leroy would stay on subject and not talk outside of his head. That only solidified what Indie knew. He'd probably been drinking since he woke up and he hadn't gotten anything to eat, either. It seemed like he was levelheaded until he said, "After he tried to kill you."

Indie laughed it off and shook his head. "You been drinking too much today, nigga? The fuck you talking about?"

Ricky walked over to Indie and Leroy after seeing the grim expression that took over Indie's face. Although Indie had laughed it off, his face turned red and his eyes danced with fury. Leroy chuckled and started mumbling to himself. He sifted through the mess in his cart, pulled his drink out and gulped it down. "I am now!"

Ricky shook his head and forced, "Come on, nigga, I got shit to do. I don't have time for this shit."

Indie held up his hand and listened to Leroy mutter. "What did you say?"

Leroy chuckled to himself and whatever other voices he heard in his head. "Who me?"

"Nigga," Ricky groaned, growing irritated.

"Yeah, Leroy, what you talking about? Fuck you mean the nigga tried to kill me?" Indie's teeth gritted together in attempt to keep his voice low.

Ricky's ears perked up, hearing the reason why Indie wasn't letting this conversation go so easily. "Oh shit."

"You were set up," Leroy shrugged his shoulders and

looked at the way Indie's face twisted and turned, soaking everything in. "He didn't know I was listening when I was walking by. No one else thinks I be listening. But I hear everything. All the time, I be listening. He said he wanted you dead. He set you up, and here you are selling his work. You got a forgiving heart, Indigo. That's why you're still alive. Because you're forgiving, but your spirit ain't right."

Indie slowly turned his head to Ricky as Leroy started to shuffle up the sidewalk past them. "They can't kill Indigo. They can't kill Indigo."

Indigo tried to sort through all his emotions, but he couldn't. "Let's go."

"You need to discuss this shit?" Ricky asked, watching Indigo walk away.

"Fuck no. I told you that somebody knew something, and I got the mind to think that everyone knew that shit."

"Leroy is a fucking drunk, Indie. You can't possibly believe shit that nigga says!"

Indie stopped and turned around to look at Ricky. "Did you know, nigga? You covering up some shit?"

Ricky instantly became aggravated that Indigo would ever question his loyalty like this. He went from enjoying his day to ready to shoot everything walking.

"Nah, why the fuck would I?"

"Because you been acting brand fuckin' new! Leroy ain't never give me a reason not to believe him. He might be a drunk, but he ain't never stole shit or lied to me, nigga. I got to believe that he was telling the truth. Why don't you want to believe it?"

Ricky huffed and said, "Because you're about to go to war with the wrong nigga."

"Apparently you're loyal to the wrong nigga." Indie gritted his teeth harder. "Get on the right side of this shit before you end up like him."

Indie let his anger get the best of him. Before this situation between him and Ricky turned for the worst, he turned around, clasped his hands together and started up the block to find Joey.

Someone else had to know besides Leroy, and since Joey was being tight lipped, he was starting there.

UNTITLED

You don't prove you're tough by shutting me out
You ain't living alone
But that's the way you carry it
Its dead, so you just bury it
It still hurts, we don't work
My heart beats every beat for you...
Melonie Fiona: Break Down These Walls

❧ 13 ❧

T aj

KICKING her shoes off by the door, she hummed softly and shuffled into the kitchen. She'd been applying for grants all week, and nothing had come back approved. Not yet anyway. She wanted to be hopeful, but she had to consider what she was going to do next. She wanted to make sure other people of color had a way into this world to do what they dreamed of.

Taj grabbed a bottle of Vodka from the cabinet and hopped on the counter. She twisted the cap off, tossed it to the side and took the bottle to the head. Drinking for her was rare, but it was a clear sign that she was stressed to the max. For a few moments, she let her mind go blank and just let the liquor flow through her veins. As she tilted the bottle upward for another swig, Malcolm's baritone brought her out her zone of nothingness.

"I thought I heard you," Malcolm's voice floated into her eardrums, making her shoulders hike a bit and tense up. "You're drinking? Is everything okay?"

Taj chewed her lip, debating if she was going to open up to him or just shrug it off like it was nothing and go on with her afternoon. His actions from the other night still lingered in her head, and she wasn't ready to talk about it.

She nodded slightly before looking up from the bottle to see him standing at her dangling feet with a remorseful look on his face. "Ali, are you okay?"

She still hadn't got used to being called anything other than Baby or Taj, but Malcolm loved Ali and called her that every chance he got.

"I'm fine," she muttered with slight irritation. Malcolm wasn't letting up. He'd had enough of the silence between them. The silence was already thick between them before the last encounter, but now it was unbearable. He wanted them to be how they were when they first met. He was determined to fix it.

Hooking her chin in his fingers, he placed a soft kiss to her lips. "No, you're not. It's probably my fault."

"Malco –"

"Ali, just listen," he spoke cutting her off. "I was out of line the other night, and I am so sorry for that. Let me make it up to you."

"There's nothing to make up, it's cool," she rebutted, but Malcolm wasn't going to take that as an answer. Taking the bottle from her hand and wrapping his hands around her, he pressed the back of her hand against his lips.

"It's not. Let's go to dinner."

"I don't want to eat."

"Ali, please."

She couldn't stand to see him beg. It irritated her more than most of the things he did. A man should never have to beg for her attention or affection. His presence would demand it alone. Deciding not to suffer through much more of his pleads, she agreed and hopped off the counter.

"Just give me a few minutes."

She had no intentions on getting dolled up. A simple dress and some sandals would suffice for this afternoon. Taj already had her mind made up to drink her troubles away, so if Malcolm wanted to take her out and pay for drinks all night, that's what was going to happen.

Malcolm was happy just to have Taj by his side with a silly smile on her face. Even if it were alcohol induced, he was going to take it. He also took into consideration that when she got drunk, she wanted to have sex, and since the other night wasn't one he was proud of, a redo wouldn't hurt.

She stumbled back into the house and Malcolm firmly wrapped his hands around her waist to steady her. Taj was in a fit of giggles, and not to mention, she was horny as hell. She turned around to kiss him and he gladly accepted her drunken affection. Her tongue wrestled his and his hands roamed her body.

Taj was aggressive, hungrily ripping him from his clothes so she could straddle his lap and feel. Feel anything that wasn't emptiness. Malcolm quickly got with the program, stripped her bare and got her in the bed so he had more room to have his way with her. He took control, and for once, he paid attention to signals her body was giving him, and Taj welcomed it.

Lip biting, ass smacking, sheet gripping, and their moans and groans filled the room. She was into it, into the feeling, the motion, the heightening of her senses. She felt like this only a few times before, and she moaned into Malcolm's ear.

"Mmm, Indie."

The second she released Indie's name into the atmosphere, her eyes shot open, and Malcom halted mid stroke and looked down at her with an envious scowl.

"What the fuck you just say?"

Taj couldn't even try to play like she didn't call her new man by the name of her old man. Malcolm pulled himself out of her and sat on the edge of the bed as Taj pulled her legs into her chest and chewed the corner of her lip.

"Who the fuck is Indie, Ali?"

With a deep inhale and exhale, Taj hesitated to answer, which was only infuriating Malcolm more. "You fuckin' another nigga?"

"No," Taj softly answered, shocked at the bass he put in his voice to ask her that. "I'm not."

"Then, who the fuck is this nigga? You callin' out his name. What's that shit about?" Malcolm popped up to his feet and started to pace the floor. The only thing he wore was socks and the condom that he hadn't pulled off yet.

"Ali, I am very patient with you. I know you got your shit you don't talk about, but there's some shit you're going to have to say to me."

"What do you want me to say?" she questioned, looking up at him. "Huh? Here's the truth. I have never stepped out on you and as long as this is a thing, I won't."

"A thing?" he questioned, propping his hands on his waist with his eyes shooting out his head. "Oh wow. What else are you going to spring on me tonight?"

"You're overreacting. Indie was my ex who died before I came to school."

"Did you love him?" Malcolm continued to question and Taj nodded. "Do you still love him?"

Taj's big eyes locked with his and swelled with tears. Malcolm didn't need to hear her answer. He knew. It made sense why she was guarded when it came to him. She couldn't give him her heart because it belonged to someone else. Dead or alive, it didn't matter. Malcolm realized that her heart wasn't his to have, but he considered trying to take it and make it his.

Running his hand over the top of his head, he looked at her and mumbled. "I can't do this."

It didn't surprise Taj. She was counting down the days before he would leave her. Malcolm grunted and shook his head. "I'm going to go clear my head. I can't stay around you right now. Not while I got to compete with a ghost of a man you still love."

"Malco—"

"Ali, don't."

He disappeared into the bathroom to clean up and Taj pushed her body off the bed, grabbed a T-shirt out the drawer and headed to the kitchen to reunite with her bottle of Vodka.

A few minutes later, Malcolm was walking out their bedroom with a duffle bag over his shoulder. "I'm going to stay at my homeboys."

Taj nodded, but didn't reply. Malcolm would have loved for her to say something, anything. But saying nothing solidified his feeling. She couldn't ever fully be his.

An hour later, Maria came over after Taj texted her with a simple, *Malcolm left*. By the time Maria arrived, Taj was showered, and back sitting on the counter, drinking the remainder of the Vodka she started on earlier. Kicking her shoes off by the door, Maria trudged over to the counter where Taj sat with an expressionless face.

"You don't look upset at all." Maria pointed out, making Taj shrug her shoulders.

With a scoff, a heavy sigh, followed by an eye roll, Taj took another drink.

"Why the hell would I be bothered? I honestly don't care."

"Taj." Maria looked at Taj oddly, wanting to know what happened, but was almost too afraid to ask her. "Why did he leave?"

"Because we were having sex and I called him Indie's name." Taj nonchalantly shrugged like it wasn't a big deal. If she was completely honest, she didn't care, and there was very little Maria could say or do to make her change her disposition.

Maria's eyes grew wide and her mouth dropped open and analyzed how unfazed Taj was with it. "Taj Ali..."

"What?"

"You called out Indie's name?"

"That's what I said."

Maria's brows met one another and her eyes narrowed at Taj's response. "You don't see anything wrong with this, Taj?"

"No. I called him the name of a man who is dead. If anything, the fact that I haven't felt anything remotely close to that until today is what we should be talking about. I'm not sorry and I don't care. If he comes back, he comes back, if not, oh well."

Maria hummed softly and sat on the counter by Taj. Maria knew that Taj's light was dim, but to see it this dim not to care or show emotion, she knew that she'd lost herself somewhere over the course of the years.

"Wow."

"Don't do that."

"I won't, but you should at least feel —"

"I don't feel," Taj admitted. "I haven't felt anything but emptiness. You know when I do feel something? During sex and I'm drunk, and that is always short lived, so oh well."

"You don't even care about how he feels?"

"Not really. Everything with him is dramatic." Taj pushed the other night off into the back of her mind, but Maria picked up that there was a lot that Taj wasn't telling her.

"Maybe if you opened up to him a little more, he wouldn't be so dramatic."

"Fuck it. It is what it is."

❄ 14 ❄

J oey

"AIGHT, NIGGA!" Joey shouted behind a car he'd just hopped out of and headed across the street to the park.

While Joey was in mid stride, he spotted Indie wrapping up a pickup game with a few of the kids from the neighborhood. With the basketball tucked under his arm, he pulled a few bills out his pocket and directed them to go get ice cream and go straight home.

Joey admired the love his brother possessed. Even if he didn't agree with anything he'd done lately, Indie was still his brother and he still had a heart of gold. But Indie was different. Joey picked it up when he saw him for the first time in years. Indie was here, but he wasn't present. There was a piece of him that was missing, and Joey could see that he was fighting just to get himself back. Just to go back to who he was before everything.

Stopping short of Indigo, Joey waited until all the kids had disbursed before he said anything to his brother.

"What, you out here being Ben and Jerry?"

"Ah, you got jokes, bro?" Indie asked with a crooked smile. "I knew you would be out here."

"What? You out here to cause a scene?" Joey asked, getting ready to turn around and walk away. "I'm not on that. I got other things to do. You need to find a damn hobby and stop bothering me."

Indie palmed his face to reset any harm that he could direct toward Joey.

"Ain't nobody here to bother you or cause a damn scene. You're going to do what the fuck you want to do anyway. But I do have some shit I need to talk to you about."

Looking at his brother oddly, Joey picked up that Indie wanted to talk behind closed doors.

"You got that look in your eye."

Joey could pick up that Indigo appeared to be calm on the outside, but his eyes danced intently with a fiery rage that wasn't going to be put out easily. Whatever Indie wanted to talk about was going to shift Joey. He nodded before looking around the courts. There were too many ears to start the conversation here. Indie threw his head toward the direction of the house and took off walking.

Joey trailed behind Indie and tried to hide the giddiness that was taking over his face. Life without his older brother had been a lot rougher than he thought it could ever be. He decided that he'd spent enough time being mad about the fact that he left and lived in the moment that he was back. Being angry with Indigo was easy, but soaking up the lessons and knowledge he had to give was going to be the hard part. It wasn't the same. Joey couldn't help but feel that there was a darker reason keeping Indie around.

Reaching the house, Indie walked in and plopped down on the couch. A rub of his hand against his overgrown, sandy curls made him groan. Joey trailed in and closed the door behind him. His brother's brow was piqued with curiosity as to what Indie had to ask of him.

The tables had turned, and Joey was now the one Indie was running to for answers. It made Joey feel wanted.

"So, what you got to say?"

Indie remained quiet just a while longer before he answered.

"You know why TK set me up?"

Indigo's question sent chills all over Joey, causing him to freeze up. Joey thought he could keep Indie away from what he knew by keeping him at arm's length, but Indie found a way around him. Joey's eyes blinked before chuckling. "What the hell you talkin' about?"

With his head tilted and his glare intensifying by the second, Joey knew that he couldn't lie about it. He wished he could. He just got his brother back, and Indie would make a wrong move and go away again, and it wouldn't be voluntarily.

"Answer me, nigga. You know why that nigga set me up?" Indie forced, staring at Joey nervously shift from side to side. Joey was so uncomfortable he didn't even realize what he was doing until Indie yelled. "Stop that shit! Hold your head up. Look me in the eye."

Indie pushed himself to his feet and took one step toward his brother and locked eyes with him. "You gave it away. You don't ever give shit away with your body language."

Joey swallowed again and took a step back and ran his hand

over his hair. The silence between the two of them were thick. Indie was going to give him a few more moments to speak up before he pulled it out of him

"Joey!"

Landing in a spot on the couch, Joey clasped his hands together and looked up at Indie, who was now leaning against the wall watching him.

"That's why I went back..."

Indie pinned his brows together and looked at his little brother. Instead of reacting, this time, he listened. He listened very carefully to what Joey had to say. Joey exhaled and said, "I went back because everything that happened that night didn't feel right. I knew that if I was in, I would hear more."

"And you heard that TK wanted me gone?" Indie questioned just to make sure he had the facts before he got trigger happy.

"I wanted to find the motherfucka responsible for putting that hit out on you," Joey added. "I wasn't ever expecting it to be TK. He showed all that love. Now that I think about it, he was just hiding his hand."

Joey nodded, and like a match to gasoline, Indie's pressure rose. "Ain't that some shit. You're loyal to snake ass niggas."

With a grunt, Joey sighed and fell back into the cushions of the couch with relief. He felt like a weight was lifted off of his shoulders now that he told Indie.

"Word was that TK couldn't let you get out and start slangin' product on your own. He said you knew too much about his business and felt like you would take over if he let you go. He knew you wouldn't come back, so he ordered a hit on you."

Indigo kissed his teeth and laughed lightly. "Yeah? Well, I'm about to know everything about his business now. I guess niggas thought that because I'm the peaceful type that I won't rain down on them."

Studying Indigo intently, Joey nodded without hesitation. He responded, "I got your back, bro. Just say the word."

Indie finally let his lip uncurl and his brows separate. "Word."

15

I ndie

AFTER LEAVING his mom's house, Indie found himself walking aimlessly down the street until he ended up on Ms. Mary's front porch. He knocked softly on the door and hoped that she didn't answer. If she didn't answer, it would mean he didn't have to deal with this feeling. But whether Indie wanted to or not, he had to deal with it. He had to face the fact that he was lost and stuck in limbo. Most days, he didn't know whether he was coming or going, and everyone needed something from him. Everyone was expecting to have the old Indie back, but the old Indie was nowhere to be found. No one knew that but Indie.

Mary pulled the door open and looked up to see Indie standing on her porch with slumped shoulders and a troubled expression etched across his face.

"Look who done brightened my doorstep. Get in here and hug me."

"You know Ricky will lose his mind." Indie forced a laugh, stepping into the house, leaning down and wrapping his arms around her.

"Why you huggin' on my momma? You got your own."

"That boy is dramatic, you know it." Mary laughed, letting him go. "You hungry? You always looked like you could eat."

Indie let her go and followed her further into the house and sat down. "Nah, I haven't really had much of an appetite since I've been back."

Mary stopped in her pursuit to the kitchen and studied Indie's face. His expression made her heart drop into the pit of her stomach. She'd never seen him like this before, and as much as she wanted to celebrate that he'd came home like he was her prodigal son, she couldn't. Everything about him had shifted and it was heavy. Too heavy for him to carry alone and too heavy for her to let him carry alone.

Mary turned around and sat in her armchair and gave him all of her attention. "What's been going on, Indigo? What's this energy you're carrying?"

He inhaled deeply and held his breath for a moment before exhaling and running his hand over the top of his head. The streets raised him to never show emotion, but right now, his emotions was getting the best of him. He was crying inside, blinded by fear, anger, and hurt and the only way he knew to express it was in anger. No one wanted to be on the other end of that trigger when he finally pulled it.

"Everything is going on. I feel like I can't get a grip on it. I can't sleep, I can't eat. I can't feel. I'm just here floating and watching everything happen around me and I can't fix it."

Mary tilted her head to the side and hummed.

"To whom much is given, much is required. Greater is He that is within me, who the Son sets free is truly free indeed. Here's what all that means. You are special. You are literally heaven sent. Everything comes easily to you, everything. But because of that, everything will attack you. Everyone will love you because of what you can do, and on the other hand, others will hate you because of who you are. You got God in you and you don't even see it."

Indie's eyes fluttered involuntarily and looked at Ms. Mary.

"And because God is in you, nothing that tries to attack you can win. Fix your crown, young man, and command these people like you were made to do. You think your life starts and ends here? No sir. You were sent here to uplift, encourage and deliver these people. Like Moses. Yes, you will fight battles. No, it won't be easy. Yes, it's going to hurt, but if God is with you, you cannot fail."

"I don't feel. I don't feel the same."

"Because you aren't the same, Indigo. You will never be the same. But you will be better, and this is how it starts. Get focused again. Get yourself out this mess and take everyone else with you. Save up enough money to buy that tech center, get you some investors and make it happen. You got it. I believe in you. Ricky believes in you. Ajai believes in you. So does your mother and your brother."

Indie scoffed, thinking about all the trouble Joey had given him up until recently. He wouldn't fault him for that, he understood. The picture was bigger than him. The purpose was bigger than him. His life was bigger than him.

"You cannot stay down forever. Four years is far too long for you to get off course. So much wasted time wasted. Too many broken hearts. It's time to walk in your purpose, Indigo. The game is going to test you."

"Never fold, stay ten toes down." Indie replied with a crooked grin and a nod. "Thank you."

"Don't mention it. You're my son, too. I love you. I'm happy you're home. Now it's time to shake it up. Get this mess cleaned up. All of it."

Mary locked eyes with Indie and he knew exactly who and what she was talking about. Taj. Indie's heart skipped a beat thinking about all the work it would take to get to her again. The idea of her with someone else made his heart pause for a second.

"I will do."

16

R icky

EVER SINCE THE party TK threw for Indie, Ricky had his head on a swivel. Indie's reappearance did exactly what he thought it would do, make the wolves put on sheep's clothing. They couldn't walk around freely anymore. They needed to hide in plain sight and what better way to do that than appear to be affiliated. Ricky wasn't feeling it. He tried his hardest to stay cool around Indie and to keep him from slipping up and really going away.

That was something that him and Joey bonded on before Joey pulled away. They needed Indie to be free. Out of hiding and not closed up in a cell somewhere. Unknown to each other, they were on the same mission to make the person causing this shit pay what they owed, even if it was with their life.

Ricky was on the way home from his mother's house and was creeping through the hood, trying to avoid the kids in the streets playing. Indie would throw a fit if Ricky hit one of his little homies, so he made sure to be as careful as he could.

"Would y'all move y'all little asses out the street, please?" Ricky said to himself, looking out the window over his left shoulder.

On the stoop of a house was a group of familiar faces. The shooters from that night. Doing a double take, Ricky waited for the kids to move out of the way before he yanked the steering wheel of the car to hit and U-Turn.

Without much thought or back up, Ricky jumped out the car and started toward the stairs. The three guys stood to their feet and watched him come toward them and point out the shooter he recognized.

"You don't even give a fuck, huh, nigga? Sitting out here like we ain't looking for you."

"Look, nigga, you don't want none of this smoke. Get the fuck off my porch," he spoke up, making Ricky's blood boil even more

Ricky hadn't shared his feelings about the shooting to anyone. He bottled it all in and promised himself that when he saw them again, it wasn't going to be much talking. But with several bystanders and no help, he quickly rethought his actions.

"Fuck all that shit. You should have circled your ass back around and made sure all of us were dead," Ricky spat, staring down at him with anger burning in his eyes. His temper wasn't what it used to be, but that didn't stop Ricky from reaching down, grabbing him by the collar and daring the other two to move with his eyes.

"Who paid you?" His words were forced through his gritted teeth and his nostrils were flared.

The shooter chuckled lightly and replied.

"TK already paid us to get rid of your boy once. What makes you think that he won't pay us again?"

Ricky's breathing hitched before jolting the shooter back into the chair he once occupied. The slick laugh coming from the group sent fire through him. He was going to handle this shit. He wanted to kick himself for not believing that TK was capable of something like this. Ricky walked away and got into his car and pulled off down the street. His head was clouded and he needed to clear it before he went home.

Gripping tightly on the steering wheel, Ricky stared at the road as his mind played that night over on a loop. It was starting to be a mashup of the night Jermaine died and the night Indie almost died. He heard the screams; he could smell the iron of Indie's blood all over him. Although Ricky had found his footing as his own man without Indie, he wasn't who he was without Indie.

That was his brother. The one that balanced him out and always had his back through anything, Ricky was indebted to Indie. He could never pay Indie back for everything he sacrificed for him. Everything Indie did to make sure that Ricky stayed out of jail hit him like a ton a bricks.

Indie didn't just save Taj's life that night, he saved his and Ajai's. Sacrificing everything to make sure that everyone around him was good was who Indie was. Ricky needed to make sure that Indie was protected and got back everything he lost that night, including himself.

Finally, Ricky pulled into the driveway and stared at the steering wheel. Picking up, he texted a shooter who didn't mind handling this run for him. Sending him the address and the details, Ricky locked his phone, killed the engine and got out the car. Shuffling to the door, he went to insert his key and turn the knob, but Ajai pulled it open with her hand on her hip.

She initially planned to chew him out, but seeing the expression on his face made her soften.

"Baby, what's wrong?"

Ricky wanted to shrug her off and shut down, but he couldn't. Not anymore. Not after everything that was running through his mind. Stepping into the house and closing the door behind him, he pressed his back against it and let a sigh out.

Ajai stood a few feet away from him and looked up at him. She knew that something was weighing on him. Something had been weighing on him for years. She thought she knew what it was but wasn't going to make an assumption until Ricky came out and said it himself.

"Baby."

"I saw him. I saw that motherfucka who shot Indie."

Ajai shuttered in fear, expecting Ricky's next set of words to include a combination of I killed him.

"Everyone who had something to do with it is done," Ricky spoke low enough to nod in agreement with himself. But Ajai heard him loud and clear.

"Ricky, it's been peaceful around here for years. Don't go turning over stones because Indie is back."

"Would you be saying that if Indie never came back? You don't get it. I lost my brother to this shit. I could've lost another brother."

"But you didn't!" Ajai semi shouted, trying to get her point through to Ricky.

Ricky scoffed and walked away from her.

"Nah, I didn't, but everything he had, he lost. That shit don't rest well with me. And I won't rest until it's fixed."

"You're being ridiculous, Ricky! I lost my dad to this shit; you think I want to lose you to it?"

"So, Taj deserved this? Did anyone deserve any of this shit? All this shit is fucking ridiculous."

"Ricky, I need you to think about this."

"I already did, Ajai."

Ajai huffed in frustration as Ricky walked to the room. "I swear there is no talking to him."

Walking into their bedroom, Ricky looked down at Bleu sleeping in his crib and sighed. He didn't find any of this to be fair. He got to live his life, have a child, build something beautiful with the woman he loved, but Indie was left with checking on Taj from the shadows. He was watching her move on without him and picking up the pieces of the life he once had. Not to mention, Indie's sleepless nights and the trauma he refused to talk about. He was his brother's keeper, and he was going to do a better job at keeping him, no matter the cost.

After almost an hour passed, Ricky's phone buzzed with a text that read, *It's done.*

❧ 17 ❧

I ndie

Now that Indie knew who ordered the hit, he decided to keep moving like nothing was different. On the outside, he seemed calm like usual, but on the inside, there was a fire burning. The more he thought about everything he went through, it only grew bigger. He was ready to unleash hell on everyone who had a hand in altering the course of his life.

He sat in the backyard with a blunt burning between his fingers and his leg bounced up and down as he stared off into space. He hadn't even heard Ajai walk out of the house. She sat down by him and took the blunt and put it out. She studied him and sighed. Her eyes dropped and looked down at her hands, then back at him.

"You're not okay. Ricky isn't okay. Something has to change," She broke the silence. "I can't lose him, and he can't lose you."

"Ajai, ain't nothing going to happen to Ricky."

"Something has already happened to him. Something happened to you. Why won't you two talk about it?" She questioned, trying to figure out why they decided to hold it in.

"Ajai, talking ain't goin' to change nothing. Action is going to change that. I don't need Ricky to get involved with anything I'm about to do."

She sucked her teeth and shook her head. "You know damn well that Ricky, Joey, hell the whole damn hood would go to war on your behalf. All you have to do is say the word, so cut the bullshit."

Indie didn't reply. He just kept staring into space.

"Do you think that revenge is going to make you feel any better?"

Indie dropped his head. "Ain't nothing goin' to make me feel better. There's a part of me that's missin'"

Ajai looked at him, inhaled deeply and scratched the overgrown hair on his face. "It's Taj."

Indie looked at her briefly before looking away. "Why don't you go find her?"

"I can't just go find her. She thinks I'm gone."

A lightbulb went off in Ajai's head. "What if I find her?"

Indie laughed. "Chill. It ain't that deep. Let that girl live her life."

"And let you sacrifice yours again and Ricky's? Nah, my son needs a father and you need to live, and this shit ain't it. So, what are you doing? You giving in or not?"

With a kiss of his teeth, he groaned and sunk further into the lawn chair.

"If you can find her, then best of luck."

"You're acting like you're okay without her. That's the furthest thing from the truth."

Indie glanced over at Ajai. "I will never be okay without

her. I will never feel the same without her. Taj took my heart. It's safe with her, and who am I to break hers and ask for mine back? That's what bitch niggas do."

Before Ajai could respond, Ricky stepped out the house. "I'm going to take care of that."

"Make sure she comes home," Indie finalized.

Indie nodded and looked over his shoulder to see Ricky standing by the door. He kissed Ajai's lips before making his way to the empty chair by Indie.

"I saw that nigga that shot you. You'll never guess who he said did it," Ricky grumbled.

"The same nigga I told you it was. Ain't no problem, though."

"What happened?"

"Nothing yet, but no worries. I don't want you involved in this shit."

"Psh. You think you doing this alone? You crazy as hell. That will never happen. We in this shit together, nigga. Say the word and you got it."

"We can't just roll up on this nigga out the blue. It's got to be the next time we drop this cash off."

"Aight, bet," Ricky agreed.

"I don't just want him gone. I want everything that nigga took from me. I'm taking over all his shit."

18

S enior

IT WAS Spades night at his sister's house. He looked forward to some real food and a few cold beers to unwind. Walking into the house, he greeted Mary's neighbor Maggy with a hug. Maggy took a liking to Senior, so Mary was sure to have her over every time Senior was around. Although Senior's heart was still owned by his late wife, Mary felt like it was time for him to move on.

"How are you doing today, Charles?" Maggy questioned after letting Senior go from her warm embrace.

"Good." Senior smiled his smooth smile that caused his chocolate face to perk up. "How about you? You're looking good."

Maggy blushed, causing Mary and Diane to roll their eyes from the small dining room table that was already set up for their game. "Thank you, so do you."

"I swear, they act like this is high school. Maggy, would you like some coffee?" Diane asked, interrupting Senior's and Maggy's conversation.

Maggy broke her focus on Senior and looked over her shoulder at Diane. "Maybe some wine."

"Well, there it goes. Chucky, take her out for a few drinks your next night off and quit all this foolishness. I got to watch y'all complement each other's buttons and peach fuzz every damn week. It's getting tiring. Come on and sit down and play this game," Mary shot her brother a look.

Senior laughed and pulled himself away from Maggy and headed toward the table where Diane and Mary were standing side by side, sipping wine and muttering to each other through their teeth. "Diane, how are you?"

"I'm great. You heard the news, right?" Diane smirked, knowing that her news would ruffle Senior's feathers. She was willing to lay it on thick, too. Just because of his disdain with his daughter and her son being together.

Senior shifted his eyes over to his sister and she shrugged like she had no clue what Diane was talking about. "What news?"

"Indigo is home. Shall we play?" Diane smirked and took a seat at the table.

Senior narrowed his eyes and immediately thought about Taj and the fact that he hadn't heard from her since she left to start her life and her business fulltime after leaving school. Now that Indie had resurfaced, the threat of her finding out that he knew the entire time was at an all-time high. Taj had been withdrawn and passive since he told her that the love of her life was gone. He knew that it would be short lived if this information made it back to her.

"Would you like to deal?" Diane's smug smirk was going to

make Senior call it a night earlier than expected. But he was determined not to let Diane get a rise out of him.

"Deal the cards while you deal with it?"

Mary groaned and shook her head. "You two need to stop it. Chucky, you can try to keep her away from here, but you know that those two will always come back to one another. You can't stop it. Don't even waste your time and try."

Senior grumbled. "Yeah, we'll see about that."

19

T aj

"TAJ, you haven't called since I left San Francisco. What's up with that?" Senior questioned as Taj struggled to juggle her purse, her computer bag, the keys she fumbled with and holding the phone between her shoulder and her ear.

"Ugh," she murmured, trying to open the door and hold on to everything, but it was no use. The phone slipped and hit the floor along with her laptop bag. Once she got the door open, she squatted down to pick up her bag and her phone.

Taj stepped into her condo and kicked the door closed behind her. She dropped the bags in a corner and dragged her feet over to the sofa where she plopped down tiredly.

"Baby, do you hear me?"

"I hear you, dad," she let out followed by an exhausted sigh. "I was just struggling to get in the house with all my shit."

"Where is Malcolm?"

"Not here," she replied. Senior was team Malcolm, and anything negative that Taj wanted to say about him, she knew that Senior would find a way to flip it around to make Malcolm sound like the second coming of Jesus. She didn't want to hear any of that today, so she decided to keep the reason behind his absence to herself. Especially since the reason he was gone was because of her and her inability to let Indie go.

Senior picked up on the irritation in her voice and it prompted him to ask.

"Everything all right?"

Taj laughed lightly. Senior was predictable. She could set her watch to him; he was about three seconds away from singing his praises.

"I really like Malcolm for you. He's the type of man you need. One with security." Senior started his usual song and dance. Taj started to tune him out and look around at everything she had to do around the house. Everything that Malcolm would normally take care of for her while she was out at work or in her office working.

"You know he's a step up," Senior's voice came back into Taj's focus, and she pulled the phone away from her ear, hit the screen for speaker and dropped it into her lap.

"A step up?" She scoffed with irritation. "Hmm...that's your take on it. But is that all you called me for, daddy?"

Senior huffed softly and mumbled something under his breath that she didn't hear, but she knew if she heard it was bound to piss her off. "We don't talk, Taj."

She huffed and dropped her head back and groaned. "I've been busy. That's why I haven't talked to you. And quite frankly, I don't want to talk to you if you're going to always talk about Malcolm. All you do is talk about him like he's the great white hope coming to save me. It's kind of annoying. Ask me how I'm doing. Ask me if I'm okay."

The strain in Senior's breathing could be heard through the speaker and it irritated Taj more. "This is what I'm talking about. You can't even make sure I'm okay."

"Are you okay, Taj?" He asked with a sarcastic undertone like he didn't want to be bothered with how she was really.

She wanted to tell him no. She wanted to tell him that she hadn't been okay for years and that she'd been waiting for him to reach out and wrap his arms around her so she could feel protection. She wanted to tell him the truth. No matter what she did to distract herself, no matter how many self-help books, how many scheduled appointments with a therapist, this emptiness wouldn't leave her. No matter how many drinks or how many times she tried to sex it away, she still felt it. Empty and desperately needing to be filled to the top with love. She needed to be genuinely loved and loved on.

Taj had refused the love Malcolm provided because she felt like he was trying to love her based on what he thought she needed, instead of asking her what she needed. Although she denied him, she missed his presence.

Malcolm wanted to make her love him by the things he did. Everything was forced, but she had to decide if she was going to give up the ghost of Indie to live life with Malcolm. He was here, in the flesh, waiting as patiently as he could to love her and receive it back.

"Baby," Senior called her name for the fourth time, pulling her out of her head. "Did you hear me?"

"Yeah, I heard you. I'm fine. I guess."

"What's going on?" Senior asked with concern. But Taj was distracted again. This time it was the door opening and Malcom walking through it with his things.

Their eyes connected and he smiled faintly at her.

"Uh...let me call you back, dad."

"Okay, Baby."

Ending her call, she watched as Malcolm dropped his bags in the room and walked back into the living area. He sat on the ottoman in front of her and took her hands off her lap and wrapped them with his.

"I didn't think you were coming back," Taj spoke up, breaking their silence. "I didn—"

"I shouldn't have stormed out like that. I thought about it and I was wrong for blowing up like that. I understand that you came into this with some trauma, and I want to help you heal that." He cut her off and took control of her attention. "You need someone who is going to love you without asking for permission to do so. I've thought about going on with my life without you, but it just doesn't feel right. I don't want to feel like that again. I want to wake up to you and go to sleep to you. I want to love you so good you'll forget about everything that happened before. I want all of you, just let me have your heart to hold. Be my wife so I can take care of you."

Taj's mouth fell open. She couldn't really process the words to say no before Malcolm slid the ring on her finger. A very faint smile crossed her face as he covered her lips with his. Malcolm's smile was wide as he stood to his feet and walked off to the bedroom. Taj nervously pulled her lips between her teeth and tried to figure out what the hell just happened.

She didn't even nod to agree with this engagement. Maybe it was a sign that it was time to let go and move on. With a heavy sigh, Taj looked at the tattoo on her wrist and quickly blinked the tears away. She didn't want to let him go, but she had to let go of the ghost of him. Indie was gone and she needed to move on. Even if she would never feel the feeling of him again, she would always know what he his love felt like.

I am so grateful that I had you... That I got to love you...To feel that infectious energy that consumed my spirit, but I got to live. I will never stop loving you. I will never forget you, but I have to let you go.

Malcolm returned with a dress and a pair of heels. "I made reservations at that restaurant you love. Get dressed and I'll be waiting."

She smiled and took the dress and heels from his hands and went to get ready. Her alone time was needed. This decision that was made for her, forced her to close a door that she wanted to leave open just in case all this was a bad dream. But the reality was that she was awake, and this was the life she was living. She had to be present for it and the people in it.

Taking one final look in the mirror, she flattened her hand over her dress. She hummed and graced the tattoo on her wrist before looking at the ring that Malcolm adorned her finger with. It was beautiful and expensive. A statement to ward off any potential threat of another man approaching her. Accepting her reality, she slipped her feet into her heels and walked out into the living area.

Forcing a smile across her face, she spoke, "I'm ready."

Malcolm's eyes danced, admiring her in the outfit he picked out.

"After you, beautiful."

M aria Sutton

"Umm Mackenzie, get this off the floor!" Maria fussed, walking into her living room where her younger sister was sitting with her legs tucked underneath her butt while pecking away on her phone. "You know when I said come spend the summer with me, I wasn't expecting you to be a slob."

"I am not a slob." Mackenzie defended, scooping up the mess she created throughout the day. "You wanted me to spend the summer with you because you missed me, which means you missed my mess."

The way Maria laughed made Mackenzie's lip curl up in disdain.

"Don't laugh. You been cleaning my mess. What's different now?"

"The fact that mama wasn't having that. Now you get here, and you forget home training." Maria smacked her lips and walked into the kitchen. "I distinctly remember there being no dishes in the sink this morning! Girl, I'm about to pack you up and send you back to mama."

Mackenzie put her headphones in her ears to drown Maria out. Frowning her face, Maria groaned and started washing the dishes and cleaning up everything Mackenzie managed to undo while she was at work. Once the kitchen was clean, Maria pulled some food from the fridge and freezer so she could make dinner for them.

Since being in San Francisco, Maria had been content with life. Not only was she close to her best friends, but she had her own place, and her peace. She couldn't put a price on that. Although, Taj had been very generous with her salary off the strength of being Taj's best friend.

Before her mind could trail off on everything she had going on, her phone started buzzing in her back pocket. Pulling her phone out her pocket, she glanced at the number and pushed her brows together.

"I don't know who the hell this is..."

Declining the call, she dropped the phone on the counter and started prepping everything. The phone went off again. This time, Maria snatched it from the counter and slid the button across the screen. "Hello..."

"Maria?"

"Yeah, who is this?"

The voice on the other side of the phone hesitated just a little. "This is Ajai. You don't know me, but I heard your name a lot from Taj."

"Ajai?" Maria asked. The name sounded familiar to her, but she hadn't heard Taj mention her name in some years.

"Ajai. Ricky's girlfriend, right?"

"Yeah." Ajai let a sigh of relief out before she continued. "I hate to call you, but I can't get in touch with Taj and I wanted to see if you could do me a solid."

Maria stopped what she was doing now that Ajai had her attention. "What's going on?"

"Well..." Ajai spoke, followed by a heavy sigh.

"Senior isn't doing well. I know he's been talking to her, but he hasn't told her what's really going on."

"What's wrong with Senior?"

"His health isn't where is should be, and he really won't do anything about it. I know it's a stretch asking her to come back here, but I think if she were here to actually lay her eyes on him, he would follow the doctor's orders. Mary is having a Labor Day cookout. Do you think she can make it?" Ajai damn near pleaded.

The mention of Senior's health and his bullheadedness when it came to taking care of himself made her groan. If nothing else, he had to take care of himself for Taj, and it was frustrating that he was letting his health fall to the wayside.

"Well... I don't think it's going to be hard once I tell her that Senior is acting a fool."

Ajai chuckled and replied with a lite sigh. "You're right about that. She doesn't play when it comes to his health. I need her to come down with all her guns blazing. He needs to be whooped back into shape."

"Oh, I'm very sure she will. How long does she need to be there? I'll need to clear her schedule."

"Hmm, if you can, clear a couple days. I think that's all she'll need to get him together. How has she been doing?"

Maria nervously chuckled and rubbed her chin. "He still has a hold on her, and she won't let it go."

"Wow. I wish I didn't lose contact with her. Could you tell her I asked about her?"

Maria nodded like Ajai could see her. "I will. I'll make sure

I'll give her your number, too. She needs all the support she can get, but you know Taj. She's never going to ask for it."

"Do you think that that's the reason why she won't let him go?" Ajai questioned.

Maria shook her head again. "No. I think that Taj didn't have the closure she needed to let him go. So, she left the door open and somewhere deep down inside of her heart, she's hoping that he will walk back in. Honestly, I adore the way she still loves him, but it worries me."

"Why?"

"Because my fear is that she'll hold on so tight to him that she won't allow herself to live her life. Ajai, for four years, she's just been existing. Just swimming through it all and not stopping to admire the things in front of her."

Maria ran her hands through her hair and chewed at the corner of her lip. "She's in a haze and just as adorable as it is, it's heartbreaking. I don't know what he did to her, but my God, four years."

"I'm hoping that when she comes back for a few days that she can get that closure she needs. You know that she didn't go to the funeral. Maybe some time at the gravesite will do."

"I hope so. Thank you for calling, Ajai, I'll get her there."

"Thank you for taking my call. I know it could've been awkward."

Maria smiled softly and said, "Listen, a friend of Taj is a friend of mine. I'll call you back with the answer."

After they said their goodbyes and Maria placed the phone on the counter. She couldn't help but feel that going back to South Central would close the door for Taj. She could fully move on with her life.

🦋 21 🦋

A jai

"So, DID YOU DO IT?" Indigo asked, looking over at Ajai who bounced Bleu up and down on her knee.

Ricky's eyes bounced back and forth, lost to the conversation. By now, he should have been used to it, but his need to always know everything and be involved was at an all-time high.

"Yep, I talked to Maria not too long ago. She's going to pass along the information and hopefully get your girl down here for the barbecue."

Ricky groaned and smacked his lips.

"Why must you ruin my eatin' ribs in peace with your light skin, R&B, baby please take me back plead?"

Ajai snorted in laughter and shook her head. "Ricky, leave him alone. He wants his girl back. He should go get her back no matter what she says or does."

"Hmm," Ricky grunted, looking at Indie with a puzzled look on his face. "What are you going to do if she has a man and has moved on without you."

"What does her man have to do with me?" Indigo asked bluntly. "Let me tell you something. She could have a man in a plane, on a train, on a boat, on a moat, in a chair, here and there but ain't no nigga going to love her and take care of her like me. I knew that I was going to get her the minute I laid eyes on her. So what I let a few years go by. That type of connection we had ain't something that dies easily. That's my anchor and the lighthouse that guides you back. Whether she thought she moved on or not, that's temporary. What we got is forever."

Ricky chuckled and stroked the hairs of his beard and huffed.

"Nigga, you are the worst! All these years. Aight...but you break her heart again and your dead in the water. She's going to kick my ass."

"Everyone better brace for impact because according to Maria, she hasn't been herself since that night, and that's completely understandable. Indie, you're my brother. I love you and all that, but you're going to have to come with more than that little ya man ain't me speech." Ajai informed.

"Yeah, that shit is weak, nigga." Ricky rolled his eyes. "That's what you were doing in Oakland?"

"Nah, I didn't have to do shit. I know that Taj is going to take a lot of work. She's different. I'm different. But if she has a man, he's not going to be around much longer."

"You talk a good game, but we'll see how you navigate through that storm when there's pressure applied." Ajai smacked her lips and flipped her braids over her shoulder. "We shall see."

"Have some faith in the situation."

Ajai and Ricky looked at each other and laughed. "Yeah. Aight, nigga."

Indigo smacked his lips and pushed himself up from the cushions of the couch. "You'll see. I always get the girl."

"Not after you lose them, though. Like you literally lost her," Ricky added his final word, forcing Indie to walk away and mutter a harsh fuck you under his breath.

UNTITLED

Been through everything, see it on our faces
Go against the grain, hundred rounds waitin'
Been around the world, hustle all places
But that '85 Cutlass in my foundation
Nipsey Hussle: One Hunnit

22

I ndie

Joey, Ricky, and Indie sat in the backyard underneath a cloud of weed smoke. They were silent, just looking into the darkness around them. To say they were nervous about their plan would be an understatement. Indie ran their plan over again in his head to make sure he dotted all his i's and crossed his t's. He hadn't found a flaw in the plan, but more so in the people he was walking into this with.

Joey and Ricky were wild cards and could easily deviate from the plan off emotion. Indie broke out his gaze and looked over at Joey and Ricky, who were sparking up another blunt. With a grunt, Indie broke the silence.

"Y'all good on everything? We ain't going over this shit again."

Joey snickered and blew a cloud of smoke into the air. "I'm cool."

"You worry too much, nigga. Let this shit be what it's going to be," Ricky added with a shake of his head. "We already covered all the bases. What else is there to talk about?"

Indie's anxiety behind this couldn't be put into words. He stood to his feet and paced the ground with his hands shoved in the pockets of his khakis.

"Nothing can go wrong tomorrow. TK moves with a gang of niggas who ain't with the shits, so I need this shit to be right."

"Nigga," Joey smacked his lips. "We got you. Chill out."

Indie winced and rubbed the scar on his chest a few centimeters away from his heart. The phrase chill out literally made him shutter in angst. Chill out. That didn't work for him. Chilling out almost got him killed. Chilling out got Jermaine killed. Chilling out was the reason he hid away in fear for four years.

Ricky looked up from his seat, noticing the anxiousness in Indigo's pace. The labored breathing and the pinned brows. Indie's outward breakdown was Ricky's inner turmoil. Looking at Indie have his moment, brought back flashbacks to Ricky that he tried so desperately to escape.

Feeling Ricky's hand on his shoulder, Indie glanced at Ricky. They shared the same painful look. The same hurt, the same fears, the same tiredness of living this life. Looking over their shoulder in fear and the threat of losing another brother to a bullet with no name. The look of stomaching the idea of taking another man's life to preserve theirs and their offspring.

"Bro," Ricky's voice rumbled and commanded Joey out of his seat. "We got you."

Indie thumbed the tip of his nose in attempt to settle his nerves, but it was no use. He clenched his eyes shut and tried to ward off the flashbacks. His body tensed up as he remembered the feeling of the first bullet piercing his skin and then the second. He remembered praying that he could shield Taj from every bullet. As the bullets missed vital organs, everything went to black.

"You're not the only one who lost something that night," Ricky shared with his hand still firmly resting on Indigo's shoulder. "You ain't the only one who is lost. I know when I told you that you needed to come home that it was for everyone in the hood, but the truth is...I needed you, nigga. I lost a brother twice. I know it seemed like I had shit together and I was holding it down. I was struggling."

Ricky now had Indie's attention. Ricky was sure to talk in an even voice; it was something he picked up from Ajai.

"All of us need you. You're a light. I put this shit on everything. You got some special shit that carry everyone, but you can't do shit until you find you again."

"And when we say chill out, it's because we got you. You had us forever. You sacrificed your life for us. Lean on us. That's what we're here for. All my life I watched everyone lean on you, especially mom after pops walked out. And you always found a way to hold it down. You always found a way to make the lights stay on, the water running, the food in the fridge. Nothing fucking phased you. No matter how many yards you had to cut, how many shoes you had to shine, how many nights you had to stand on the street corner. You're that nigga. Can't nobody in this hood say otherwise," Joey spoke up proudly with his finger pointed at his brother's chest. "You nigga...it's you! You made the set proud, you made momma proud, shit you made me proud. There ain't shit you're going through alone. Look at us. This is family. This right here is a bond made of blood, sweat and tears and we ain't letting you down. Not this time. Hold your head up."

The emotion flickered in Indie's eyes as they bounced back and forth from Ricky to Joey. Without permission, Indie let the tears roll down his cheek, but he didn't wipe them. He embraced them. He embraced the only life he knew and the promise of a new life on the horizon. He embraced who he was now, and where he was going.

"You ain't alone under these dark clouds, nigga. They perfect for us. They mean the sun is on the horizon. We walking into the rays, nigga," Joey spoke up, placing his hands on the back of Indie's neck and pressing his forehead against his.

Indie grabbed the back of Joey's neck and clenched his jaw tightly. Without saying a word, they all thanked each other. If everything failed tomorrow, they would know that their brotherhood stood the test of time. They needed this. They needed each other.

The next morning came and the day inched by until the sunset and it was time to handle the business at hand. The three of them sat across the street and waited until most of the traffic in and out of TK's place died down. Indie didn't really care about who saw them. He was more concerned about innocent bystanders being hit by any stray bullets that were bound to ring out.

"You good?" Ricky asked, killing the engine.

Indie nodded and swung the passenger door open.

"Yeah, I'm cool. Let's get this shit over with."

On command, the three of them walked across the street and up the narrow driveway into TK's place like they would any other night they were bringing him money. TK's security relaxed seeing Indigo walk through the door with Ricky and Joey behind him.

"Fuck you niggas going?" Manny's rough voice rumbled, seeing the three of them walk in. Although Manny seemed like he was going to give them a hard time, he didn't care. TK had been working them from sunup til sundown. Any fucks he had to give was out of the window.

"Damn, y'all deep tonight, huh?" Rico grunted, looking at the scowl on their faces. "Go ahead and head in."

Indigo looked at Rico and Manny standing by the door and disdain was smeared across their faces. He stopped for a second. "Manny, you good?"

Manny kissed his teeth and scoffed. "I'm tired as fuck, but what that got to do with anything?"

"You got a baby on the way I heard. You know the streets be running their mouth. Congratulations, nigga." Indie ignored Manny's sore comment and focused on Rico for a second.

Rico smirked for a second before dropping it. "Yeah, right now actually. Her mother just called me."

"And you here?"

Rico shrugged his shoulders. "You know how this shit goes. Business is business."

Indie shook his head. "Look, both of y'all hang tight for a second. I'm going to holla at TK about some work and see about letting y'all out of here early, aight? Do me a favor, though, get everyone out of here."

"Aight, bet," Rico nodded, letting the three of them go without a pat down or a raised brow.

Strolling into TK's office, Indigo sat down in front of his desk and looked at him. The goal was to come in and take everything he owed them, but Indigo had a sudden change of heart. He needed to look in TK's face man to man.

TK looked from his phone and twisted his expression.

"Fuck you niggas doing walking in here looking like the remix of NWA? Fuck you want? It ain't drop night."

Indigo chuckled and looked back at Joey and Ricky standing by the door. "Ricky kind of does have that Eazy E vibe without the AIDs. Rest in peace."

Indie turned back to look at TK, who now had his gun placed on the desk, but Indie wasn't moved by the gesture.

"All jokes aside. I needed to run some shit by you."

"That ain't protocol."

Indie chuckled again. "I ain't worried 'bout all that shit. TK, do you lose sleep? I do. I ain't slept right in four years. Shit ain't been resting easy on me. That night plays on a loop every time I close my eyes. I like to think I was a likable nigga. The type that niggas around here respect, so it's unclear why someone would want me gone."

"We having a therapy session or some shit?"

"Nah," Indie snickered. "Not at all. More like clearing my conscious. So, like I was saying before you cut me off. I was thinking and I put my ear to the streets. You were the only one to benefit from me being out the way. Because without me, it would be chaos, which is cool."

TK watched Indie stand to his feet with confusion etched across his face. He couldn't understand why he was so calm about knowing that he was the one that ordered the hit. TK laughed it off and scoffed. "We done?"

"Nah. Not yet. An eye for an eye, a tooth for a tooth. I'm just getting started."

The lean that TK had been sipping throughout the day was prohibiting him from reacting fast enough to pick up his gun. Indie grabbed his from his waist band and pointed it at TK's chest. "You should've made sure I was dead. Should have had those driver's circle back around. Should've told them not to miss my heart."

Joey and Ricky had their guns drawn, ready to rain down on him, but Indie had everything under control. Without batting an eye, Indie fired one bullet into TK's chest, making his heart stop on impact. "I'm the heart of this city. You can't kill that shit."

Ricky opened the door and looked at Rico standing on the other side with his gun drawn. "What the fuck!"

"Everyone gone?"

Rico nodded and tried looking over Ricky's shoulder. Ricky pushed him back with the barrel of his gun and said, "Go assist your baby mama. We'll be in touch."

"Manny," Indie spoke up, stepping out of the office while wiping the barrel of the gun off.

"Get rid of him and go home. I'll see you in the morning. And if anyone asks you about shit, tell them to come find me."

23

J oey

ALMOST A WEEK HAD PASSED since the transition. Joey and Ricky were concerned that there would be push back, but there wasn't any. Everyone who'd been working with TK for years had easily dealt with his absence and fell into line with what Indie had put into place. Only a few days after assuring that TK was disposed of properly, Indie met with all the runners and discussed his plan with the company. He made it very clear that the goal was to get off the streets. None of them had a reason to question Indie. And no one was going to question him now that he removed TK. They would blindly follow Indie off a cliff. That's how Joey knew that Indie was it.

Counting the money and stacking it up on the table, Joey looked over at Indie, who had just finished making sure that everyone was paid exactly what they were owed and nothing less.

"Remember that building you were looking at?"

Indigo nodded and took a seat. "What about it?"

"We got enough to buy it, furnish it, and get this shit off the ground," Joey informed, making Indie's ears perk up.

"The STEM Center? I still need to line up a few investors and find out who is running that shit while this shit is going on?" Indie already knew the answer, but he needed to see how dedicated Joey was to this.

Joey scoffed and looked at his brother. "What you mean who's running it? Me!"

Indie started laughing. "You ain't ready to get out this life. Why you playin' and wastin' my time?"

"Ain't nobody wastin' your time, Indie. I'm serious."

Leaning back in his seat, Indie studied Joey's face and nodded. "You got to separate yourself from this shit. I'm not taking nothing away from you because I'm proud of the man you became without me. I can't lie. It hurt me to know that you fell into my footsteps when I left. There's shit about me I want you to pick up and there's shit about me that I want you to let die."

Joey pushed the money to the side and drummed his fingers against the wooden table. With his free hand, he rubbed the top of his head and focused on the wall. There was unspoken emotion building up in his chest and he didn't want Indie to see it. He'd done a great job of burying it away. "You're like pops."

Indie scoffed and started to tell Joey to fuck off, but Joey spoke up again. "Like my pops. I am the man I am because of you. If it wasn't for you, I would be far worse off. You're more than my brother. I picked up everything. I watched you. I damn near wanted to be like you. I wanted to be mad. I wanted to hate you because I didn't understand back then. It seemed that everything I thought was good, you took away. But really, you were protecting me. Not like I was your brother, but like I was your son. I ain't tryin' to get emotional about this shit. I just need you to know that I will do whatever, go wherever, and move however you require me to move."

"It's love, JoJo." Indie laughed, calling his brother by the nickname Taj gave him. "Forever love. Ain't shit going to change. Secure the building and let's get this shit moving. Joey, do not fuck this up."

"I'm not going to fuck this up." Joey assured, studying Indigo's face. "You miss her, huh?"

"Miss who?" Indie played it off like his mind hadn't been flashing on Taj all day.

"The girl you stole from me. The one of my dreams." Joey chuckled. "You need to get her. What's all this worth if you don't have your girl by your side."

"When you get so damn smart?"

"I've always been smart, nigga. You just taking notice."

"Don't say nigga, nigga." Indie grunted, standing up.

Joey followed suit and started putting the cash in the safe.

"But you heard me. You're about to be out this shit for real. Go get her back before it's too late."

"I hear you, bro."

"Yeah, hear me all you want. If you don't get her, I will."

Indie kissed his teeth and chuckled before walking out of the room.

"Keep talking crazy."

"Quit being scared!"

24

Taj

"Ugh." She groaned, walking into the bathroom and unwrapping her hair. She let her silken tresses fall from the wrap and grace her bare shoulders. Since the engagement, she hadn't slept much, mostly due to her trying to dig deep and find all the emotion she pushed away. "I'm freaking tired."

Inhaling deeply and exhaling, she picked up her comb and combed her hair out. She stared at the ring for a second. "Taj, did you say yes?"

Before she could reply to herself, the buzzing on her phone in her pocket was a needed distraction. Pulling the phone out, she looked down at the L.A. number and hummed. It was familiar, but with iPhone's latest update, she caught on to the tiny print under the number.

Maybe: Mama Diane.

Drawing her neck back, she hesitantly answered the phone before she was sent to voicemail. "Hello."

"Well, if it isn't Taj Ali herself."

Taj couldn't fight the smile taking over her face. Her heart fluttered and she felt warm. Just the mere sound of her voice stirred up emotion in her gut.

"Mama Diane, how are you?"

"I'm making it. You would know if you called, but I see you threw me away," Diane sassed.

Taj laughed a bit before replying.

"I didn't throw you away. I just thought that you were tired of hearing from me and needed time to go without... you know, thinking about him."

"Mmm, little girl." she chuckled. "You mean you needed time to stop thinking about him. How has that been working out for you?"

"Honestly?"

"Honestly..."

"It hasn't, but every day, week, month, year that creeps by, it seems to get easier. Or maybe I'm used to it."

"I know what you mean. Just because he's gone doesn't mean I'm going to let you go," Diane spoke up. "Mary is having her annual bash and you should come home, just for a week. Let me feed you and show you where we laid him. Close that chapter."

Taj paused for a moment before replying, "I don't know about that."

"Just think about it for me. I would love to see you. So would Ricky and Ajai. Y'all have so much to catch up on."

Taj nodded like she could see her make the gesture and chewed at the corners of her mouth. "I'll consider it but..."

"I'm not going to keep you long. I just needed to hear your voice. No matter what happens in this life or where you go, you will always have somewhere to call home with people who love you. Okay?"

"Okay," Taj spoke softly, staring at the blue tattoo on her wrist. "I'll talk to you later."

"I won't hold my breath, Baby. I love you."

"I love you, too."

❀

THE GRANTS they applied for was rolling in back to back, and she finally had a few people and companies requesting her assistance, but none of them piqued her interest. They were all bland with no purpose, and people looking for a handout without pouring back into their community. Deciding to focus on the grant applicants later, she sat back in her office chair and looked at the ring that graced her finger.

Malcolm indeed had done a great job. She just wasn't sure that this was the path she wanted to travel. The rest of her life was a long time not to have a love so mind-blowing and stirred a fire in her soul. She'd been battling herself with this engagement for a minute and still really hadn't found any resolve. One thing she did know was that she had to make a decision. She was either going to choose herself or choose him. Whatever choice she made, she had to live with.

Lost in the trance of the diamond dancing on her finger, she almost dove off deep into the realms of her mind before Maria opened the door and walked in. Snapping back into reality, Taj looked up and cleared her throat. She smiled faintly as Maria closed the door behind her and took a seat.

"I thought you had a flight to catch with Mackenzie to North Carolina?" Taj asked, looking at the expression on Maria's face and the folder in her hand. "What's wrong?"

Maria sighed and sat up and slid the folder across the desk toward her. "I got a phone call from Ajai."

Taj's eyes shot open. "Ajai?"

"Yeah. She looked me up and decided to call to see about you."

Taj pushed her brows together in confusion. With a tilt of her head to the side she spoke. "Why did she need to see about me?"

Maria rubbed her fingers over her chin and looked at Taj. "Because you cut everyone off when you left. And just because you tried to forget them, doesn't necessarily mean that they forgot you."

"That's all she called for. Just to check in?"

"No, she really called because in typical Senior fashion, he refuses to take care of himself. She was hoping that maybe you should come home this weekend and see about him. You know, make him do what he's supposed to do."

Taj rolled her eyes and groaned. "I swear Senior is the worst about his health. Mom used to put his vitamins on the counter right by his keys and his coffee. That was the only way she could make sure he took them until she found out he was sliding them into the trash can."

"So, he's always been a pain in the ass?" Maria chuckled lightly.

"Always and forever." Taj sighed, thinking about her mother. She hadn't given her much thought, but that didn't stop her from missing her. Her smile, her touch, her lessons and her guidance. She needed her mother's guidance right now.

"I had no plans for Labor Day, so I guess I can go."

"That was easy."

"Diane called me today."

"Indie's mother?"

Taj nodded. "She told me about the cookout my aunt is doing and gave me the guilt trip."

Running her hand along her face, Taj groaned, letting Maria catch a glimpse of the rock on her finger.

"Umm, excuse the hell out of me! What is that?"

Taj flipped her hand over to glance at the ring like she hadn't been staring at it almost all day.

"An engagement ring."

"I can clearly see that. When did he ask and why didn't you say anything?" Maria was visibly upset the Taj hadn't shared the big news. Taj, on the other hand, was looking for emotions to convey that she was slightly okay with it. She was looking for some indicator that this was the direction her heart was pulling her in.

"Don't be upset, it happened fast. I don't even think I verbally said yes." Taj shrugged it off and opened the folder to find a plane ticket.

"I guess you aren't leaving much of an option?"

"No, especially not anymore with that rock on your hand. You're finally moving on. It's time to get some closure." Maria's face had now gone from irritated to reassuring. "Close that door so you can open up a window. Let the sunshine and happiness take over again."

Taj snorted and nodded. "Thank you. Get out of here. You have a plane to catch. I will see you when I get back home."

Standing up to hug her, Taj held her a little tighter than normal before letting go.

"Thank you, Maria."

"Anytime. Please enjoy yourself."

"Of course."

Just as soon as Maria walked out the door with her things with the last set of employees, Malcolm walked in with a bouquet of flowers. She thought that she at least had time to figure out how she was telling him that she was going back to Los Angeles for a week.

"Hey, beautiful," Malcolm smiled like it was Sunday morning and he got some early morning booty with French toast on the side.

"Hey," she spoke, pushing her freshly blown out hair out her face. "I wasn't expecting you."

Taking the flowers from his hand, she hugged him and forced herself to be in the moment and feel something while taking his feelings into consideration. "Thank you."

"Anything for you," Malcolm replied, taking notice to the plane ticket sitting on her desk. "You going somewhere?"

His face twisted a bit until Taj reached out and grabbed his hand. She had to attempt to consider his feelings, and although she wanted to weather this storm by herself, she had to extend the invitation and prayed that he would say no.

"Senior isn't taking care of himself the way he should, and I need to go see about him."

"Anyone else you plan on seeing?" He questioned, feeling uneasy about her return back to L.A.

"Whoever I see I guess. Do you want to come?"

He nodded. "Of course, especially if this is going to offer you some closure."

A faint smile took over the frown her lips were trying to form.

"Okay, we fly out tomorrow, so we should go and pack."

"After you."

When Taj got home, she had a feeling that she was on the verge of something. A strange feeling overtook her and she couldn't seem to shake it off or hide it. She stood in the middle of her closet with her hand on her hips, staring at her clothes waiting to be packed.

"You good?" Malcolm rumbled from behind her. She shrugged, unsure of how she felt.

"I haven't been back in years. I just ... I don't know."

"It'll be fine. This is your opportunity to let all that baggage go and move on. Get the business together, start planning this wedding and focus on us."

Before Malcolm could touch her, she shifted and started to pull her suitcase off the shelf.

"I suppose."

Malcolm instantly became annoyed. "Look, I'm going home with you because you need the support to get over this thing you've been holding on to for years. But I advise you to get excited about this, baby."

Taj scoffed and rubbed her forehead. "Let me focus on my father and I'll focus on everything else. Okay?"

She didn't wait for him to reply. She shut down and concentrated on packing her clothes, seeing Senior, and finally letting Indie go.

❧ 25 ❧

I ndigo

"WHEW, THAT BITCH IS CLEAN!" Joey shouted as Indigo stepped out his new Lincoln Continental. "You an OG deep down, huh? Most niggas go out and buy a Benz. You got a Lincoln like you 76."

Indie chuckled and shut the door. "You ain't know I was an OG? Urban legend my nigga. She clean, though, without a doubt. Where is, Ma?"

"Inside, humming and cleaning like she got company coming over," Joey shared, walking around the car. "Where is mine?"

"You got paid, right?" Indie asked, climbing the stairs to the front door. "Go get you a car and get the hell out of moms house, nigga."

"Don't say nigga, nigga," Joey joked, opening the driver's side door and hopping in the front seat. "This shit is fresh!"

Chuckling lightly, he walked in the house and the smell of Pine Sol and Pledge hit his nose. The last time she cleaned like this, their grandmother was coming from Louisiana to visit. Being that she'd been gone for over ten years, Indie knew she was getting ready for someone else to visit.

"Ma!"

"This house isn't that big enough for you to be hollering like that. What's up?" she asked as she appeared from the hallway with a dust cloth in her hand. "What brings you over here?"

"I was hoping you had food cooking or something. What you been up to?"

Diane finished dusting off a few pieces of furniture before putting the cleaning supplies away and sitting down. "I'm not cooking nothing. You could have picked me up something."

"Nah, I'll just take you to dinner." Indie shrugged, taking a seat. "Why are you cleaning like this?"

"Because I wanted to. You look put together," Diane said, looking her son up and down. Indie's hair was freshly cut, he looked rested and his clothes weren't baggy, but neatly put together.

"A little birdie tells me Taj is coming home."

With his eyes squinted, Indie focused on his mother and chuckled a little bit. "The bird's name is Mary. I can't help but wonder what you did with that information."

"I can't help but wonder how you're going to get her back in your good graces. Because if I were her, I would be livid."

"So, that's why you're in here cleaning like you got a man coming over here. You called her. Didn't you?"

Diane shrugged innocently like she hadn't been known for meddling in his business before. "I don't know what you're talking about."

"Ma," Indie groaned. "Please, don't tell her nothing. She needs to hear it from me."

"You're damn right she does. You ever thought about the possibility of her showing up with a man on her arm?" Diane presented Indie with his worst fear. "You expect her to stop her life for you after you removed yourself from hers?"

"You right, but I can guarantee that any sucka she's with is a weirdo and doesn't know her how I know her."

"You mean, how you knew her. Four years, son. That girl you used to know is a grown ass woman now, and you're going to have to put in some real work if you want her heart back."

Indie groaned and ran his hand over his face. "I didn't come over here to think about this. I came over here to take you out."

"Well, you better think about it. She'll be arriving tomorrow." Diane pushed herself up from the couch and started off down the hall. "Where are we going?"

"Dinner. In your car." Indie smirked. "Hurry up, girl!"

"Boy!" Diane shouted before closing her room door.

Before he could really get deep inside of his head, Joey walked in with a smile on his face. "That shit is really nice."

"Sure is, too bad you ain't driving it. Put the word out that I want everyone to chill tonight and tomorrow. Enjoy their families. Give everybody some extra. I don't want no shit to pop off. I don't have time to be cleaning up shit."

"You nervous?"

"As fuck," Indie responded.

Joey smirked and leaned on the wall. "It'll be cool."

"Yeah, it will."

"All right, enough talk about business," Diane interrupted them, walking back down the hall with her purse in hand. "I don't want to hear that shit. Let's go."

Indie popped up from his seat and chuckled. "Joey, I'll see you tonight. Take care of that shit."

"Watch your damn mouth." Diane groaned while walking outside. Her tone quickly changed when she spotted the new car sitting in her driveway. "You bought yourself a new car?"

"Nah." Indie smirked, tossing her the keys. "I bought you a new car. We got reservations."

UNTITLED

Where your backbone, nigga, where your code at?
Where your down since day one real bros at?
Where them stories you tellin' unfold at?
Where your heart, nigga? Where your soul at?
Nipsey Hussle: Perfect Ten

T aj

"WHAT PART of Los Angeles is this?" Malcom questioned, stepping out of the Uber and looking around.

Taj scoffed and rolled her eyes before pulling her phone out to send Maria a quick text. She was letting her know that they were here and that Malcolm had gotten on her nerves the entire way. His comment from the other night was still rubbing her the wrong way. All Malcolm seemed to want was her to himself, but he had yet to ask what she needed. As open as she was trying to be, her heart wasn't allowing him to pry its door open.

Inhaling the air, she released it and looked up at Mary running out the house and down the stairs to greet her. "Crenshaw."

For a moment, she stood frozen on the sidewalk with her mind flashing back on that night. This same spot. The blood stain was out of the pavement now, and so was her heaviness. She used to tell herself that she would never come back here because she didn't want to face this again. But amazingly, she felt his presence all around her and it was peaceful.

"This is home, where my heart rests. Where I'm not in pain. The only place that I feel...us. Him...again..." Taj mumbled to herself, letting one tear fall from her eyes. "Indigo, I miss you so much."

"You know we're not staying here, right?" Malcolm asked, looking around in disgust, breaking her out of her trance. She tucked a piece of this energy she felt for later because Malcolm was bound to piss her off in some form or fashion. "I'm booking us a room."

Taj ignored his mini meltdown about being in Crenshaw more than five minutes and gladly welcomed Mary's embrace.

"Oh, Baby!"

"Hey Auntie," Taj smiled, holding her tightly. "I missed you so much!"

"I missed you, too. Look at you, still skinny as ever." Mary pulled back to look at her before noticing Malcolm. "Oh, you brought your ... friend."

Malcolm was exchanging some words with the Uber driver and handling a phone conversation at the same time.

"What is he doing?"

"Trying to book a hotel in the city." Taj rolled her eyes and prompted Mary to do the same.

"Uh, no sir. Get those bags and bring them in the house. You two are staying here with me. He can sleep in Ricky's old room," Mary announced. She didn't care how grown Taj was. As far as she was concerned, Malcolm wasn't getting his rocks off inside of her house with her niece. She was confused as to why he was here. This week was family, and he was not family.

"Ali, we aren't staying here," Malcolm spoke up. "We'll come back after we get a room."

Mary held her hand up and shook her head. Taking a few steps toward Malcolm, she stopped at the trunk of the Uber.

"I said you're staying here with family. Get her bags and bring them inside. You're not afraid of being in the hood, are you? I've never met a man afraid of some graffiti and a stray bullet. Tighten up, your slip is showing."

Mary gave him a once over before smirking and taking a step back. "Taj, I got some food and a bottle of wine. Ajai and Ricky will be over tonight to see you."

Taj looked back at the look on Malcolm's face and traveled inside of the house behind Aunt Mary. "Your dad will be over in the morning. He's working."

"As always."

Taj walked into her old room and noticed how Aunt Mary left it the same way she had it before she went off to college.

"I couldn't bring myself to change it. It was Jermaine's room and now it's yours. You put life back into it."

Malcolm wobbled into the room holding all of Taj's bags and his. Aunt Mary's lip curled upward while looking at how disoriented he was trying to bring all the bags in at once.

"Just put her bags in the corner. Your room is down the hall."

"I'm not staying down the hall." Malcolm spoke up as though he had a choice.

Taj shot him a warning glare before Aunt Mary chuckled.

"He's funny, Taj. I give you that."

"Ali, we're staying in the same room or we're going into the city." Malcolm made it sound like a demand more than an option. Normally, Taj remained silent, but she was home and safe from anything that he could do or say.

"No, I'm staying in here. You're down the hall in Ricky's

old room," she repeated, staring at Malcolm. His shoulders were squared and hitched to his ears as he dropped her bags by the door. "Want me to show you?" Taj asked.

"No need. He's a big boy. It's the second on the left," Mary directed.

"I'm going to get some work done. I'll let you have your family time," he grumbled, walking off down the hall.

Taj placed her hand on her forehead and groaned. "I'm sorry about that, Auntie."

Mary watched Malcolm disappear and shook her head. "You know it's okay to ride them and leave?"

Taj chuckled and ran her hand down her face before Mary grabbed her hand and stared down at the ring.

"Shit," Taj blew. "I meant to leave this at the condo."

Mary pulled her into the kitchen and grabbed a bottle of wine. "We're going to talk about this. Why didn't you say anything?"

Mary poured them both a glass and sat at the table. Taj took a long sip and mumbled into the glass. "Because there wasn't anything to say. He asked and I didn't answer. I'm engaged. It was rather quick and I ended up drunk that night."

"Baby," Mary shook her head in disapproval. "This ain't it, this ain't. That is not the man for you."

Taj placed her head in her hands and groaned again. "There was only one man for me. I can't have him back, so I'll take what I get."

"So, you're going to settle? Really? Let me guess. Your daddy has something to do with this, doesn't he?"

Taj slowly nodded. "He loves him. Malcolm is all he talks about. I don't want to disappoint him again. You know? I feel like I've done enough to him."

Mary scoffed and waved her hand in the air.

"Baby, this is going nowhere fast. You know it and I know it."

"Where is my cousin!" Ricky burst through the door and Taj quickly took her ring off her finger and put it down her shirt into the cup of her bra.

Cutting Mary a silencing glare, Taj finished her glass and said, "In the kitchen."

"Whew chile, this is going to be a mess."

🕸 27 🕸

R icky

"You look skinny as hell!" Ricky hugged Taj tight before kissing the top of her head. "I'm about to fatten you up."

"Try as hard as you can. I can't keep weight on to save my life. Where is Ajai?"

"She'll be by tomorrow; she had a lot of shit to take care of today. And why can't I spend time with you without an audience?" Ricky chuckled letting her go. "Talk to me. What's been going on with you?"

"Nothing really. Work and more work. What about you? Still running around here with your trigger finger itching?"

Ricky shook his head. "Shit shifted. You want to take a ride with me?"

"Does where we going involve food?" Taj rose her brow, making Ricky laugh.

"Hell yeah. Ma, you want something?"

Mary shook her head and waved them off. "I'm going to see Diane anyway. You two go have fun."

Taj didn't even give a second thought to Malcolm in the room, sulking about not staying in a hotel in the city. He could stay there and sulk. She was going to ride around the hood with Ricky shotgun and hold on to the peace she felt earlier.

Taj was silent for the most part, letting the wind grace her skin as Ricky gripped the steering wheel and headed toward a taco truck a few blocks over.

"Baby, how you been?"

Ricky broke their silence as he pulled into the parking lot where the taco truck was. "You don't call, you don't write. What the hell is going on with you, girl? You still with that sucker?"

"That sucker is here," Taj replied with a sigh. "I've been trying to just find my footing as me right now. I guess I've been holding on to this idea of what if."

Ricky put the car in park and looked at his baby cousin fiddle with her thumbs.

"What if?"

"What if that night never happened? Where would I be right now? Maybe happy, not faking it just to make it, but for real happy. I've been chasing that feeling. Are you over it?"

Ricky threw his head toward the door, motioning for her to get out the car. Following suit, she climbed out and followed Ricky to the window to order some tacos. Ricky threw his arm over her shoulder and ordered for the both of them before he answered her question.

When they were sitting at the table nearby, Ricky said, "Nah, I ain't over it. First, I lost Jermaine. and then I watched Indie go. A nigga got real PTSD living in the hood and that shit transferred to you by association. Watching the love that grew between you and him was magic, and I never got a chance to tell you sorry. Sorry that I didn't do a better job of protecting the family. I was a wild card back then. All I thought about was myself and what I was feeling right then. Never about the what if. But now, I can't stop thinking about the what if."

"What changed for you?" Taj asked with a mouth full of taco contents.

Ricky smiled bright and wiped his hands off.

"Bleu...my son."

"Excuse me!" Taj covered her mouth as she gasped. Swallowing the rest of her food, she smiled wide. "Why didn't you tell me?"

"Ajai wanted to tell you, but then she felt bad because the space surrounding us was hazy. Honestly, I felt guilty as fuck that I had my piece of happiness and yours was ambushed and taken away from you so fast and repeatedly."

Taj smacked her teeth and waved him off.

"Ricky, it didn't matter what space I was in mentally or emotionally. I missed y'all and I felt that same haze. I was so stuck on what I was feeling, I didn't even think about what y'all were feeling. You know this is a damn shame."

"That it took us four years to have this conversation?"

"Exactly. Can we promise that we won't do that again?"

Ricky smiled faintly at her. Knowing that what was happening tomorrow would send her into a spiral, he nodded, taking the promise lightly.

"Ball in your court, Baby. I've been waiting on you."

"Here I am." The smile on her face was genuine. "I thought that coming back here would make a mess out of me. It's like I feel his peace. He's around."

"He's around, all right," Ricky mumbled before changing the subject. "Does that nigga make you happy?"

"What's happy when you work all the time?"

"There's my answer. Don't waste your life with that sucker."

"I heard Aunt Mary and I hear you. I just have to go about my own way."

Ricky stopped and examined her. "He's not hurting you, is he?"

"Nah," Taj quickly answered. "Everything is cool. I just don't love him and I'm trying to, but it ain't working."

"If you're doing this for Senior, scratch that, I know you're doing this for Senior. That nigga has lived his life and still is, and you're miserable. You should have never moved away from us, Baby. You know we don't allow this shit."

"I know, I know."

"Do that shit for you. Don't be afraid to step out for Taj Ali. You're the truth. It's in you, not on you. Make that shit shake."

28

J^oey

HOPPING OUT THE CAR, Joey threw his hand up to the driver and climbed the steps and sat down. The sun had set and the last of the errands Indie had him run were complete. He could just sit back and relax. Diane was over at Mary's house and Indie was at Ricky's, getting his nerves together. Everyone involved with their business was at home with their families or hanging out but for the most part, it was quiet. This was the quietest it had been in years and he welcomed it. Welcomed the opportunity to relax his mind. If the rest of the weekend was going to be like this, it was going to be a good weekend.

For a minute, he had a moment to dream and be an eighteen-year-old. Inhaling and holding it in for a few minutes, he released it and smiled. Although his dreams of playing football had left him years ago, he could still put his best foot forward. Indie planted a seed in his head earlier and didn't even know it. For the last four years, Joey saved up most of his money, waiting for this time to come. They were making strides to really get out this time, and they had the money to get out and take everyone with them.

Looking for the right building to kick start Indie's dream sparked a flame inside of Joey. Not only did he get the building, he bought two more. One to flip into an office building and the other for Ricky to do whatever he wanted to do with it. Half of the strip mall was theirs, and if all went well, the rest of it would be, too. Joey leaned back on the steps and softly chuckled and reflected. The pieces of the puzzle were coming together, and every emotion they went through to get here was finally making the bigger picture worth it.

A chirp of a siren broke him out of his bubble of happiness. Looking up to see a cop car stop in front of the house, Joey raised his brow and watched as the cop who rode on the passenger side whistled and waved him over.

Joey chuckled and shook his head. "Y'all know better than that shit. What you want, nigga?"

"Joey, I'm white." the officer spoke up.

"My eyes work fine. Like I said, what you want, nigga?"

The officers chuckled amongst themselves. "Have you heard from TK? We've been looking for him for a minute."

Joey's face remained neutral as he shook his head. "I don't work for that nigga no more."

"But you're down with the set."

"And what that got to do with TK? There's a hundred niggas wearing blue from here to Overhill. What's your point?"

"You used to. Where is he?"

Joey groaned. "Is something wrong with you? Are you hard of hearing?"

"Indie know where he is?"

Joey sat up to get a better look at them. "I doubt it. Indie don't fuck with this shit no more. Now, y'all have a great night."

With that, Joey stood to his feet and walked inside of the house. "They out of their damn minds."

29

T aj

HER SLEEP WAS PROBABLY the most peaceful it had been in a while without Malcolm in the bed next to her. She even slept in without interruption. Walking down the hall toward the living room, she pulled her hair into a ponytail and hummed to herself. It was amazing what being back in Crenshaw was doing for her. Although there was pain that lingered, the love from her family overtook that feeling.

"She's finally up from her beauty sleep," Ajai's voice clashed against Taj's ears, making her spring down the hall. She dashed to wrap her arms around Ajai. "I missed you so much! I am so sorry I didn't call and check on you."

"I am so sorry I didn't call and check on you! You look great! Where's the baby?" Taj wasn't letting Ajai go and neither was Ajai. Ricky couldn't help but laugh at how the two of them didn't miss a beat.

"With my mom, they'll be here soon."

Finally, they let each other go just to stare at one another and wipe tears from each other's face.

"Y'all are ridiculous." Ricky chuckled. "Y'all didn't even miss a beat."

Ajai smiled and held Taj's hand. "True friendship doesn't die. I'm happy you're back."

"You know, so am I. I'm here all week. We have so much to catch up on." Taj said before the front door opened.

"Hey!" She heard Senior's voice rumble through the front door. "Baby!"

Taj's face twisted into a smile before she let go of Ajai's hand and rushed over to Senior. She wrapped her arms around Senior's neck.

"Hey, daddy! How are you!"

"This is a surprise," he spoke into her neck, lifting her off her feet slightly. "Why didn't you tell me you were coming?"

"Because you would have told me to stay in The Bay. But I have a bone to pick with you. A little birdie told me you haven't been taking your medicine. I have no plans on burying you, so please do right, daddy." Taj shot him a warning glare and he couldn't help but smile, seeing his daughter's spunkiness start to peek back through.

He was so excited to see her that he forgot the one reason he didn't want her back here. He knew it was a matter of time before Indie waltzed through the door and sent the calmness Taj had out the window and replace it with fury. A fury that would be unmatched to anything she'd ever felt or anything he'd ever witness.

"Baby, you could have told me that over the phone. I know I have to do better, but you didn't have to come all the way here to do it."

It was too late anyway. She was already here and there was

nothing he could say or do to make her turn around and go home. He only wished he had been privy to this information before she got on a plane to see him.

This had Diane's name written all over it. After that twisted expression she gave him the other night, he knew she was behind this. No one championed for Taj and Indigo the way she did. No one applied pressure for him to tell Taj the truth like she did. But Senior just couldn't do it. Telling her about Indie would mean that their relationship would be over.

Taj had finally come around to Senior, and he didn't want to lose that. Taj tilted her head and looked into his face and asked, "Where did you go just now?"

Clearing his throat, he said, "I'm just happy you're back."

"I'm happy to be back. I didn't know I would feel like this but, it's good. How has work been? And everything outside of work because I know there's something going on. I can sense it."

Taj fell into the couch and crossed her legs. "Tell me or have me find out. I'm here all week."

"All week?" Senior damn near passed out.

"Yeah, all week. I have some doors to close." She huffed. "Like going to the gravesite and actually saying goodbye so I can—"

"Ali!" Malcolm bellowed down the hallway. She could sense his irritation and it made her tense up. Senior raised his eyebrow before he smiled.

"You brought Malcolm with you?" Senior beamed almost like he was more excited to see him than he was to see her.

Ricky poked his head around the corner and pushed his brows together.

"Who the fuck is he calling like that? Nigga got to take all the bass out his tiny ass voice."

"Why is he calling her Ali?" Ajai questioned, watching Malcolm barrel his way into the living room.

"Why isn't your ring on your finger?" He questioned, holding her engagement ring between his fingers.

Laying his eyes on her, he curled his lip at the sight of her in a loose-fitting tank top and a pair of distressed jean shorts. Pulling his eyes from her to Senior, he cleared his throat and straightened up.

"Mr. Adams, how are you doing?"

"Ring?" Senior asked with a smile. "Y'all got engaged?"

"Engaged?" Ajai's eyes popped out her head and looked at Ricky before clenching her teeth together. "Ricky..."

Ricky silenced her with a look. Indie made him swear not to say anything about him to Taj before he could explain himself.

Taj rolled her eyes slowly and caught Mary's disapproving glare from the kitchen.

"You can say that."

Malcolm stuck his chest out proudly and tenderly took Taj's hand from her lap and slid the ring back on her finger. Kissing her cheek, he mumbled in her ear. "Don't take it off again. And find something else to put on."

Pulling away from him, Taj stood to her feet and shook Malcolm's attitude off. Senior grabbed Taj's hand and admired the ring that Taj didn't want anything to do with.

"You don't look happy about it, Baby."

Malcolm clenched his jaw and looked at her. "She doesn't seem too excited about marrying the man of her dreams."

Ricky scoffed. "That's because you ain't the man of her dreams. You're a weirdo."

"Fuck you just say to me?" Malcolm questioned like he stayed up the better part of the night rehearsing that very line.

Taj pushed her brows together and frowned her face at Malcolm's rehearsed line of How to Survive Crenshaw for Dummies.

"You heard him," Ajai spoke up, folding her arms over her chest and looking at Malcolm like he was enemy number one.

"Baby, why aren't you happy about this? Malcolm is a great guy," Senior started.

Taj was burning. The calmness she felt was quickly going away. Senior was pressing her with questions surrounding the engagement she never agreed to. Malcolm and Ricky were exchanging words and Malcolm's mouth was writing a check that his ass couldn't cash. Ricky might have calmed down, but he would still come out of pocket for Taj any day, at any time.

Mary caught on to Taj slowly slipping back into her shell and shouted.

"ENOUGH! This is enough! Ricky, stop it. Malcolm take a corner. Everyone take a damn corner! Taj and Ajai help me in the kitchen. Ricky, go for a walk. Malcolm and Senior, start the grill! This is a damn shame."

Ricky glared at Malcolm as he made his way out the door. "You in my hood, nigga."

"Yeah, okay," Malcolm scoffed, following Senior out of the house.

With the separation of everyone, the mood had come back to neutral. Ajai switched gears and started catching up with Taj while they finished cooking the food.

"Did I miss the party?" Diane asked, walking in holding a bowl in her hands. "Ricky is outside smoking like a chief."

"Let's not even talk about it." Mary huffed before looking at Diane, who shifted her eyes to the door.

Taj spun around and smiled at Diane as she dried her hands off. Mary took the bowl from Diane's hand so the two could embrace. Holding on to Diane, Taj inhaled her scent and sighed before letting a few tears fall out of the corners of her eyes.

"It's okay," Diane whispered in her ear, holding on to Taj as tight as she could. "It's all okay."

Diane pulled away to wipe the tears from her face and the door creaked open slowly. Ajai and Mary looked at each other nervously as Indie stepped in and stared at Taj. She was looking at his mother with eyes full of remorse.

It only took Taj a second to glance up at him, look away, and connect her eyes with him again. Diane still held on to her as her knees weakened. The look on Taj's face was indescribable. For a few minutes, Taj stared at him in disbelief. Ricky stepped in the door behind him and she knew it was real. She wasn't dreaming. He was really standing there looking at her.

Covering her mouth, Taj screamed into her hands and buckled over. As hard as she tried to muffle her scream, it escaped between her fingers. It alarmed Senior and caused him to run into the house. Taj struggled to stand up and wept. She looked at Indie, and then at everyone around the room.

"What is this?" she asked while Ricky nudged Indie forward. "What the fuck is this?"

"Baby," Indie spoke up breathlessly, getting closer to her. Taj warded him away, shaking her head. "I didn't want to leave you."

"No," Taj spoke up. "No. You're. This isn't real! You're not supposed to be here. What kind of sick ass joke is this? Do not come near me!"

"It's me, I'm real." Indie started talking again.

Diane stepped off to the side so that Indie could close the gap between them. "I am so sorry."

"Four years," was all Taj could manage to say.

Malcolm stepped inside the house behind Senior and pinned his brows together. Taj didn't acknowledge that her fiancé was standing less than five feet away from her and her former lover. "Four years? You had...you all ... y'all knew?"

"I told them not to say anything. Baby. I couldn't do it." Indie reached out and wrapped his hands around her wrist. On contact, she felt that spark. The shock of electricity that laid dormant ignited again. Her brain couldn't process it. Yanking away, she pushed him and turned to Senior.

She could scream at Ricky, Ajai, Mary and Diane, but Senior was the one she trusted to shield her heart from this type of pain.

"You fucking knew! You knew and you didn't say shit to me! You didn't even give me that option to choose! Fuck what he did, but you dad! You are the only one I expected to be honest with me. Not them, but you! And you fucking failed again. You've let me down three fucking times!"

Taj was inconsolable. The volume that her voice raised to had everyone shook. Senior looked at his raging daughter and swallowed the lump in his throat and said, "It was for your own good. You would have followed him."

"IT WAS MY FUCKING CHOICE TO MAKE!" She screeched. "Mine! No one else's but mine, and you took it from me three times. You're dead ass wrong. Fuck you! It was never about me. It was about you and the control you wanted to keep. I'm done. You're dead to me."

"Baby," Indie spoke up once more.

"Ay, man, she told you no." Malcolm stepped up, finding this to be the perfect time to step up and defend Taj, but she wasn't here for it. He was a day late and a dollar short. "Fall back."

Indigo didn't pay Malcolm any mind. Instead, he followed Taj out the house and down the steps. "Get the fuck away from me! Fuck you. Had me going crazy and praying that I could have just said goodbye, and you were alive and living your fucking life! I haven't lived in four years, Indie! Four years!"

"Just let me explain—"

"There's nothing to explain to me. There is nothing you can say." Taj took off down the street and pulled her phone from her back pocket to get an Uber to the city. She needed to process all of this alone.

UNTITLED

Police hit the light's, that's a car chase
Lookin' back at my life make my heart race
Dance with the devil and test our faith
I was thinkin' chess moves but it was God's grace
Nipsey Hussle: Higher

❧ 30 ❧

I ndie

"Fuck!" Indie shouted, climbing in his mother's car to go search for Taj. "Fuck! Fuck! Fuck!"

Gripping the steering wheel as tight he could, he searched up and down the block for her. He was going to check every hotel in the city until he found her and explained himself. He knew that she was going to be pissed off, but he never expected this. Taj was beyond pissed and it was going to take a lot of work to get her back on his side.

Driving toward the city, Indie mumbled to himself. He was trying to find something that would make sense to her. Anything to make her just stop for a minute and listen to him. But words failed him. There was nothing he could say, but the same spark she felt back at the house, he felt it, too.

Just as Indie was about to get on the freeway, his phone

started to go off in his pocket. Hoping it was Ricky with some news about her whereabouts, he fished it out. He answered it without looking at the screen.

"What?" He spoke.

"So, you must know," Rico grunted.

"Know what?" Indie asked.

"Joey just got hooked up for distribution," Rico hesitantly announced. The news made Indie hit the steering wheel.

"What the entire fuck! I thought I told you niggas no work! No work means just that! I don't fucking care if it was a gang of fiends! Who fucking told him to do that?"

Rico didn't want to answer. It was very rare that Indie's voice raised, but it was almost just as loud as Taj's was.

"He did it on his own."

"You got to be fucking kiddin' me! Got damn it, Joey!"

Pressing the gas petal to the floorboard of the car, Indie took off toward the county jail. "I got to deal with this shit."

"Indie," Rico spoke up. "That ain't a wise idea, nigga."

"Why the fuck not?" Indie questioned.

Rico groaned. "It's better if you get a lawyer to go in and advocate because the cops have been asking about TK and asking about you."

Indie let up off the gas and dropped his head back against the headrest.

"Aight, I'll take care of it. I don't want no one to move until I say so."

"I got you," Rico said before disconnecting.

Indie was going to take a shot in the dark and call the lawyer that got him off a distribution charge years ago.

"Indigo Sims," he answered. "Never thought I was going to hear from you after you told me you were going straight. What's going on?"

"Bobby, it's not me this time... it's my brother. He's down at county. I need you to work your magic and get him home."

Bobby sighed and cleared his throat. "All right. You know my fee."

"You know I'm good for it."

"All right, I'll call you soon."

Indie hung up and pulled off the freeway and drove until he reached the beach. Parking the car, he got out and stood in front of it, trying to calm his nerves. He couldn't. His head spun. Between Taj running off and Joey getting arrested, he couldn't get himself to calm down. All he could do was just try to breathe and put out one fire at a time. Joey was now a priority, and Taj would need some time to calm down before he could talk to her.

Almost an hour went by and he got a call from the county jail. He leaned on the hood and answered it.

"What's going on?"

"I fucked up. Bobby is bringing you some papers. Indie, let me sit on ice," Joey shared and Indie's pressure shot up higher.

"No, nigga, you stupid you won't—"

"My bail is a mill. Build up these businesses before getting me out of here. I'm cool. I got myself in this shit and you can't save me from everything. When you get those papers from Bobby, you'll know what to do."

Indie closed his eyes and pinched the bridge of his nose and exhaled. Joey was right, and Indie knew he was.

"Listen, I'll make sure money is on your books. If you have any issues, just call me."

"Every boy has to become a man some time. I'll be cool, aight? Just make the set proud, nigga."

Indie dropped his head and let a few tears fall from his eyes before he replied.

"Aight, nigga. Don't be saying nigga."

"See you soon."

"Before you know it."

Indie waited for Joey to hang up before dropping the phone and looking up to the sky. Gathering his emotions, he picked his phone up and called Ricky. Ricky only let the phone ring a few times before he answered.

"You found her?"

"Nah, we got bigger shit to worry about right now."

"Like?"

"Joey got hooked up for distribution and these cops are looking into TK. Tomorrow, I want to have a meeting. I'm turning up the heat."

"Aight, I got you. I'll have Ajai find Taj."

Indie grunted and shook his head as if Ricky could see him.

"Nah, let her cool off. She'll come back when she's ready. Or I'll go to her. Just give her a minute."

"If you say so. I'll get up with you. Hold your head, nigga."

"Aight." Indie nodded again and hung up. "Two steps foreward, six steps back."

Indigo stayed put a little while longer after getting a text from Bobby, asking him where he wanted to meet him. Dropping his location, Indie stared out into the distance, waiting on Bobby to pull up.

Almost an hour later, Bobby pulled up beside Indie with a folder in his hand. "I'm assuming you talked to Joey."

"Yeah." Indie nodded.

"This charge carries a ten-year sentence minimum. There are a few details that are sketchy. But I'll work on it. And while I do, you work on this."

Indie took the folder from his hand and looked at three deeds and the contact information for a tech company out of the Bay area.

"BOLDnBLUE...Ali Sims. Got damn, JoJo."

Indie smirked and thanked Bobby for his help. "I'll have that money to you in the morning."

THE END, For Now....

AFTERWORD

"The game is gonna test you, never fold. Stay ten toes down. It's not on you, it's in you and what's in you, they cannot take away."

- Nipsey Hussle The Great

Jessi, Shajuana, Ivy, and B. Love, thank you.
Domo and Sid, thank you.
BLP, thank you.
SMDII & SMDIII, thank you.
Family and friends, thank you.
Loyal readers and new, thank you.
Everyone who said, no, thank you.
I'll see you between the pages.

The Marathon Continues.

ALSO BY AUBREÉ PYNN

Thank you for reading! Make sure you check out my catalog:

Dope Boys I&II

Everything is Love

Mistletoe Meltdown

My Love for You

My Love for You, Always

Say He'll Be My Valentine

The Way You Lie

The Way You Lie: The Aftershock

Run from Me

Love Over All

The Game of Love

Love Knockout

Fight for Love

All to Myself

All to Myself: Love, Power, & Respect

Coldest Summer Ever: A Collection of Poetry

Indigo Haze: Thug Love is the Best Love

Color Me, You

SumWhereOvaRainbows: A Collection of Poetry

Connect with me on my social media:

IG: @aubreepynn

TWITTER: @aubreepynn

Facebook: Aubreé Pynn

Check out my website:

Aubreepynnwrites.wordpress.com

A million words, in a million books, is never thank you enough for your support.

CPSIA information can be obtained
at www.ICGtesting.com
Printed in the USA
LVHW041933211019
634862LV00004B/909/P